# Darkness Before
## the Dawn

D1605576

# *Darkness Before the Dawn*

## Belle Reilly

RENAISSANCE ALLIANCE PUBLISHING, INC.
Austin, Texas

ISBN 1-930928-06-8

Second Edition

First Printing 2000

9 8 7 6 5 4 3 2 1

Cover design by Mary Draganis

Published by:

Renaissance Alliance Publishing, Inc.
PMB 167, 3421 W. William Cannon Dr. # 131
Austin, Texas 78745

Find us on the World Wide Web at
http://www.rapbooks.com

Printed in the United States of America

For the Beetles, who are known but to me.
Your unflagging encouragement, assistance and support helped to  make this
possible.  Love ya!

— Belle

# Chapter
# 1

**Manhattan, New York: March 30, 1999**

So what if it was four lanes away and going in the wrong direction? It was yellow, it was on duty, and it was empty. In the chilly, slushy New York afternoon that had followed a morning of intermittent snow, it was golden.

"TAXI!"

Screeeeech!

"Where the fuck ya goin'?"

More braking wheels and blaring horns.

"Asshole!"

The battered cab she'd hailed swerved recklessly across the oncoming traffic, skidding to a stop about ten yards past her. As it swept by, only her quick reflexes saved the tall, dark-haired woman from being doused by the wave of sludge kicked up by its wheels. The travel bag she'd slung over her shoulder and the flight kit she carried didn't help her balance any, but she had survived worse than this.

*No tip for this jerk.* She shook her head and warily made her way up to where the driver had wedged his vehicle behind a bottled water delivery truck.

In spite of her luggage, she knew better than to expect the cabby to lend her an assist. She could see him through his partially rolled-down window, tamping out the cigarette he'd been smoking, and bobbing his head to a beat only he could hear.

*Great.* She pulled at the balky door of the cab and angrily shoved her bags inside. She was running late. She'd spent more time than she'd intended on that damned letter. She reached once more into the pocket of her dark blue trench coat, feeling the folded envelope, reassuring herself that it was still there.

It was.

Another horn blared as she cast a glance up at the steel gray clouds overhead. The snow wasn't over with yet, she knew. She gathered her coat against the cold and breathed in the bone-chilling air that carried the stink of exhaust, burnt rubber, and disappointment.

*It won't be much longer now,* she reassured herself, sliding into the back seat.

The driver pivoted slightly, wordlessly raising his eyebrows and swabbing a finger under his runny nose.

*Two can play at this game,* she thought, silently returning the favor, with a piercing, questioning blue gaze of her own.

Neither of them blinked.

She was tired of all this crap, tired of New York, tired of having to fly busloads of yammering passengers to all points on the compass; they could sit here the rest of the afternoon for all she cared. It was up to the beat-bopping cabby.

After he'd locked eyes with her for several seconds, she could see the sullen demeanor of him evaporate, and he folded. He'd been beaten fair and square, and he knew it. She was the boss, as if there had ever been a doubt.

"Where to?"  He returned his attention to the road.

"JFK.  Orbis Airlines."

"Traffic's pretty heavy goin' that way."  With herky-jerky stops and starts, the driver maneuvered the cab back into the flow of cars.

"Get me there before 4 o'clock and I'll make it worth your while," she said, turning to the right just in time to see a transit bus nearly broadside them.  The cabby was oblivious to it all.

"Yes, ma'am!" he said, punching his foot on the accelerator.

Captain Catherine Phillips settled back into the shadowy interior of the cab.  It would be a wild ride to JFK, she was certain of that, as the cabby tried to salvage the possibility of a good tip.  She closed her eyes.  She would make it to work on time after all.

*Work...*and that's what it was to her.  Flying had long ago stopped being the thrilling, exhilarating love of her life.  Now, she imagined herself as no more than a glorified tour guide, barely along for the ride.  Oh, she was a professional —more so than most of her colleagues, she considered—but that was because of her training, her character.  She didn't know any other way to live. Wasn't capable of it.

But soon...she idly fingered the letter in her pocket—she would be done with it. After this last haul to Rome and back, she was quitting. Leaving the people-moving business to others. She would take that job with Federated Parcel, moving cargo that didn't talk back. That was the answer, she was sure of it.

*Just like you thought quitting the Air Force was the answer...*Catherine popped her eyes open as the cabby suddenly jammed on the brakes.

"Sorry," he said, looking anxiously into the rearview mirror.

*Will wonders never cease?* the pilot thought. *An apology from a New York cab driver. For that alone, this guy gets his tip!*

"We're almost there," the cabby said, and indeed, in the sky outside the smudgy window she could see an L1011 suspended in the air like a Christmas ornament, initiating its final approach for landing.

"Almost," she whispered, though she knew it wasn't true. Her breath lightly fogged up the glass as she watched the plane descend.

No.  To Captain Catherine Phillips,
it all had never seemed so very far away.

\*\*\*\*\*\*\*\*\*\*

The Hilton courtesy van veered
sharply to the right, horn bleating, forcing its way into the outside lane of traffic heading towards the Kennedy airport
departures loop.  The van's occupants,
six men and women wearing various
dark blue and white combinations of the
Orbis Airlines flight uniform, lurched to
the left.

"Geez, buddy, take it easy, will ya?"
A young man of medium build, with
close-cut dark hair, narrowly dodged a
spray of coffee that came slopping out of
his half-lidded Styrofoam cup.

"Sorry!"  The driver threw up his
hands defensively.  This was his fourth
trip to the airport so far this day, and his
dispatcher had already radioed him that
there was another full load—airport
bound—awaiting his return to the big
hotel in Manhattan.  Great.  He'd be late
for dinner again.  His wife would have
his head.

Nathan Berbick sourly noted the
driver's apology.  "And keep your hands
on the wheel while you're at it!" he said,

returning his attention to his coffee cup. He lightly massaged his temple as he carefully took a sip of the steaming mixture. "Ahhhh..."

In the momentary silence, a voice piped up from the back of the van. "I begged him not to drink that last kamikaze!" and all the occupants, save for one moderately hung over flight attendant, roared with laughter.

"Nice, Alan," Nathan's voice was stony. He blearily eyed his chipper, sunblonde colleague. "And it was a Jell-O shot, if you must know!"

"Like you could even tell the difference at that point!" Cindy Walters gave Nathan a playful nudge in the ribs, causing him to once more cradle his coffee as if it were a baby. "I'll tell you, Nathan, if word of that show you put on gets back to the desk jockeys, they're liable to put you up next trip in the Hoboken Motel 6!"

"I didn't hear you complaining last night!" Nathan said with a smirk. He teased the petite brunette, knowing she could take it.

"That's because you fell asleep," she blandly replied, and she turned her face to the window.

Once again, laughter erupted throughout the van, and eventually Nathan and Cindy joined in. They'd had an on-again, off-again "thing" for the past year or so; as of the previous evening, it was distinctly "on" again, much to Nathan's delight.

Cindy put up a sharp-tongued, quick-witted front, but Nathan fancied he knew just what buttons to press to get the Southerner to reveal the softer, nurturing side of herself that he so...liked. He'd nearly blown it last night, he knew, but she'd promised as they packed their flight bags late this morning that she would give him another shot at it during their layover in Rome. *If* he vowed that he'd lay off the *grappa* this time.

"Man! The traffic is crazy around here!" Alan Ross's hollow voice again floated up from the rear of the vehicle.

"I just wish that American Airlines strike was over," a forty-something red-head sighed. Joan Wetherill, the first flight attendant, peeked around Nathan's shoulder to look through the front window of the van. "And that US Airways slowdown in a show of support—ugh!"

They were approaching the terminal drop-off area. The place was a madhouse, complete gridlock. It appeared to the older woman as though the jam-up was more of a chain reaction accident, what with occupants abandoning their cars, taxis, and shuttles, arguing over who was at fault. They were still at least half a mile from the Orbis gates.

"Tell me about it," said Joan's seatmate, Trish Dugan. "I'm sure our flight will be packed with a lot of happy passengers...*NOT.*" And she grimaced at that horrid thought. The flight attendant had been working with Orbis since forever, or so it felt to her. She was bored with her job and tired of battling both the airline's corporate politics and her own conflicted desires. At this point, she didn't think she'd ever make senior crew or lose that extra ten pounds. Just the thought of those harsh realities threw her into despair. No matter that Rome lay at the end of the rainbow, this was going to be a long flight, indeed. And even longer on the return shift she'd pulled.

"Who else is crewing with us, Joan?" Cindy swiveled around in her seat to face the older woman behind her.

The senior flight attendant shook her head. "You're looking at it."

"What?" Trish's voice was a near-screech.

"Oooh...you've done it now, Trish. She's awake at last!" Alan Ross reached a tanned hand to the young, blonde-haired woman snuggled next to him. "Becky?" Gently, he gave her shoulder a quick shake.

"Huh?" It was obvious that the girl was slightly disoriented. Then, catching herself, her green eyes snapped open to full alert and she self-consciously moved away from Alan's side.

"We there yet?" She groped for her flight bag.

*Darn it, Hanson!* she chastised herself. She'd fallen asleep again. Was no place sacred?

It wasn't as if she hadn't exited early from the revelry in the Hilton's bar. No, she preferred to leave the more dedicated partying to her coworkers. Particularly on the eve before an overseas haul.

She'd been teased about it since she was a child. She was quick to nod off, slept like a stone, and greeted the dawn of each new day with eyes that refused to prop themselves open, requiring at least two hits of the 'snooze' alarm. And now, to have found herself unintentionally slumbering against the blue trench coat of Alan Ross...she feared it would be the stuff of his dreams for weeks.

"Sorry," she said, a blush flaming her cheeks.  She averted her eyes from her grinning friend.  *And why weren't they at the airport by now, anyway?*  She turned to look out the rear window.

"Hey, take it easy there, Champ!" he laughed.  "I don't mind you keeping me warm!"

"Alan!"  Cindy called back from the front bench seat, "Keep those hands of yours in full view at all times!"  She smiled back at the still-confused Rebecca Hanson.  "He botherin' you, hon?"

"No more than usual, Cin," she replied, finally getting her bearings.  She gave her fellow Californian a playful shove and smiled up at him.  "I'll keep you posted."

"Joan, what do you mean we're it?" Trish Dugan persisted.  *How was it that this flight from hell kept getting worse?* she wondered.

"Orbis has laid on extra flights to accommodate passengers stranded by the strike," Joan explained to her now attentive flight crew, "so staff is running lean and mean."

"Emphasis on the 'mean,' it sounds like." Nathan drained his coffee cup.

"Ah, maybe it won't be so bad after all," Becky rationalized, running a finger through her short, feathered hair. "If we stick together, it'll be okay..."

"Are you kidding?" Trish was nearly slumped double on her seat. "I ran into a friend of mine yesterday after we landed. She was working the 108 from LAX to Atlanta, and she told me she had two passengers start slugging it out in the stand-by line. They had to call the cops!"

"Oh my gosh!" Becky's face blanched.

"Ah...we won't have to worry about that today, Champ." Alan put a calming arm around her shoulder. "See, it could always be worse."

"Obviously," Nathan pointed out, "you haven't heard who our pilot is this trip."

Cindy started tightening the belt of her coat. The Orbis Airlines terminal entrance was creeping into view at last. "Isn't it...Joe somebody? That cutie from Santa Fe?" She knew her comment would get a rise from her dark-haired friend, and it worked.

"No," Nathan said testily.

"Who, then?"    Trish's voice was fearful.

"It's 'Frosty the Snow-Bitch.'"

Collective groans issued from everyone but Joan and Becky.

"Frosty?" Becky asked. They'd lost her on that one. But it wasn't the first time and it probably wouldn't be the last. The young flight attendant from southern California had advanced quickly through the crew ranks at Orbis, and so she frequently found herself on the more preferred routes with far more seasoned colleagues. At times, she thought, they seemed to be speaking in a language of their own that eluded her, and she wondered more often than not whether it was just as well.

She loved her job and loved working hard, making sure every last detail was attended to. Nothing pleased her more than being there for her passengers, being responsible for them. In a sense, for however many brief hours they were together, they were like family to her, and they made her miss her own not quite as much. Even through all the peanuts, pillows, and barf bags, she loved every bit of it.

And the same could be said for her colleagues, she considered, as she looked up at the blonde Adonis sitting next to her. Alan Ross was a poster boy for 'LA Surfer-hunk,' no doubt about it. With his barely cut-to-regulation sun-kissed hair, blue eyes and brown skin, she knew there was no reason why she shouldn't be falling at his feet. Still, for all the flirtatious bantering that passed between them, she thought of him strictly as the big brother she'd never had.

Becky hadn't worked the 2240 from JFK to Rome more than a few times, and she was relieved to see that Joan Wetherill was senior this trip. She'd taken an instant liking to the older redhead several years ago when they first crewed together on a trans-con JFK-LAX run. She had appreciated then how Joan had looked out for her and shown her the ropes. Not to mention how the senior flight attendant had backed her up when a certain first class passenger had a few drinks too many, and took it upon himself to put his hands where he shouldn't have on Becky's person.

To this day, Becky wasn't quite sure what Joan had said to him, her voice was so low and her face so close to his as she spoke. But it had proven effective, and the offensive passenger elected to snooze the rest of the way to LA. No, if there was one thing one didn't want to do, it was to get on the bad side of Joan Wetherill or to tangle with one of her charges.

"Captain Ice Cube!"

With a start, Becky realized Nathan was still talking, earnestly trying to have her "get" whom he was talking about.

"Catherine Phillips," Alan whispered in her ear. "A real piece of work."

"She pissed me off so much last year on the 196 to London—I swear I thought she was gonna hit me!" Cindy Walter's face flushed at the memory.

"And it wasn't even Cindy's fault!" Nathan supported his sometimes girl-friend.

"She could hit *me* with her best shot, I'll tell you!" Alan said, and they all laughed at that.

*CatherinePhillips*...Rebecca thought. She had never flown with the pilot before, but she certainly knew of her by reputation. In the crew circles in which she traveled, it was a name that was feared and reviled. Most of the talk had to do with tales involving the captain's fiery temperament. Fortunately, she'd never heard any indictment of the pilot's flying skills. Becky tried to turn a deaf ear to all the gossip and innuendo she'd heard about the former Air Force Academy graduate, preferring to make her own judgments about a person's character. Well, today, she would get that chance where Captain Phillips was concerned.

She only hoped she survived the experience intact.

"All right kids, dial it down a notch, will you?" Joan rebuked their bawdy laughter with a stern gaze. 'Captain Frosty' or not, a captain was still a captain, and that demanded a certain degree of respect. She'd flown with Kate Phillips a number of times and found her to be a demanding professional, exhibiting an economy of word and motion that the senior flight attendant marveled at. Do your job, do it well, and the pilot had no quarrel with you. As a result, the two had established a working relationship that was efficient, civil, and collegial.

And with Catherine Phillips, Joan thought, that was as close as the pilot would ever allow herself to step towards the line of friendship. A line that for her was bold, clear and intractable. Never to be crossed. And some small part of Joan considered that a shame...for the captain, more than anyone else.

The driver tooted lightly on his horn several times in quick succession, and Becky realized that the forward crawl of the van had slowed to a complete stop.

"All right, this is as close as I think I'm gonna get you folks," he said glumly, pushing up on the bill of his Yankees baseball cap. They were still nearly forty yards from the Orbis entrance, and idling virtually in the middle of the congested access road. "I could try to work it in a little more, but that might take another 10 minutes and..."

"And we could get there and back again on our hands and knees in that amount of time," Nathan cut in, leaning towards the sliding door. "Thanks a lot, bud."

Nathan shoved open the door and hopped out onto the slick macadam, turning back almost as an afterthought to help Cindy and the rest of the women behind him. With resigned sighs, the flight crew piled out of the van and into the bedlam of a strike-mired JFK.

They ran a gauntlet of traffic, winding their way into the terminal; Nathan looked back and noticed with some satisfaction that the Hilton courtesy van was now boxed in.

"Ladies..." he said, standing to one side and waiting with Alan while the four women slipped through the revolving door of the terminal. Just inside the entrance, the group paused to get their bearings.

"Anybody for a quick cup of coffee before we go to the lounge?" Nathan glanced towards the escalator, and a Starbucks coffee sign.

Cindy linked her free arm in his. "Let's go, sweetie. Last call."

"Ahhh..." Alan's blue eyes lit up at the prospect of more caffeine before take-off.

"Go ahead," Joan laughed. "I'll take care of checking us in at the lounge. Catch up with you at the gate?"

And with a few quick nods, the group split up, Becky and Trish trailing behind Joan. They began wading their way through the mass of travelers, dodging rolling bags, tour groups, and scrambling children. It was pandemonium, that was for certain, with no signs of improvement anytime soon, at least until the strike was settled. It was painfully apparent that the overflow of travelers was stressing Orbis' resources to the limit.

They kept to the perimeter of the crowds as best they could in an attempt to avoid the heaviest traffic.

"Oh God, there she is!" Trish Dugan hissed. She gestured towards the next set of revolving doors street-side.

Rebecca followed Trish's gaze and saw what had to be the most striking woman she had ever seen. Her figure was partially obscured by the long regulation trench coat she wore over a pair of dark blue Orbis slacks and a dress jacket. But Becky could tell that she was lean and tall, taller than most of the people around her, and her long, rich black hair was pulled back and plaited behind her. Her 30-ish features were fine and strong, and twin laser-blue eyes scanned the terminal from beneath the bill of an Orbis Airlines captain's hat. Becky was amazed at how serene and calm the woman appeared in the midst of the surrounding chaos.

The young flight attendant pulled up short, startled, when the captain's eyes settled on her own for one second, two at the most. The hard stare told her nothing about the woman and, just as quickly, the moment was over and the pilot had moved on.

*Wow...that is one cool customer!*
Becky thought, losing Captain Phillips
in the crowd. They would meet up
again, soon enough. Perhaps Phillips
had recognized her as being with Orbis,
and that accounted for the stare.

"Don't worry, Becky—she doesn't
bite," Joan said, casting a reproving look
at Trish Dugan.

"That's not what I heard," the heavyset woman sniffed. She tugged on her
wheeled suitcase, sneaking a sidelong
glance at Becky. "I'll bet she has peeps
like you for breakfast!" and she barked a
sarcastic laugh at her own attempt at
humor.

Joan narrowed her eyes at the caustic
flight attendant. "Gate 22," she said.
"Let's get going."

\*\*\*\*\*\*\*\*\*\*

He was just a businessman, an Italian businessman, moving in concert with
the stream of passengers pressing
towards the security checkpoint. He carried an expensive black woolen coat
over one arm, and in the other he held a
soft leather bag: a briefcase doubling as
a carry-on. He wore a charcoal double-
breasted suit, Moschino of course, with a

custom-made white cotton shirt, and a red tie dotted with flecks of green, the better to bring out the emerald of his eyes. Pine-pitch colored Fermani lace-ups completed his ensemble, and with some satisfaction, Roberto Andizzi noted they were nearly the same dark color as the stylishly trimmed curls upon his head.

"Don't draw attention to yourself," Stefan had warned him, "but don't try too hard to disappear in the crowd—for that will surely arouse suspicion. You look the part. You have a right to be there, as much as any other first class passenger." The ethnic Albanian had clapped him on the back. "You look good!" He had said and given him a cold smile.

The cheap hotel room, in a dive so close to the airport that planes overhead had rattled the windows all night long, was shabby and cold. But when Roberto had turned to Alexandra and seen the appreciation in her eyes as she took in the sight of him wearing the expensive clothes—so foreign to a man of his military background—his heart had warmed. He was doing the right thing. He knew it. The tall, beautiful woman with the high Slavic cheekbones had him under her spell, and he would do anything for her. The fact that he had even agreed to Stefan's plan—was poised even now to put it into action—wasn't that proof enough to her of his love?

As the security checkpoint loomed ever closer, Roberto told himself that it was for her that he'd agreed to brazen his way onto a big jetliner, carrying the unassembled pieces of the latest in high-tech, non-metallic firearms. Not for Stefan, not for the Kosovar's friend Mishka, but for his Alex. Soon this mess would be all behind them, and he and his black-eyed beauty would be together. Ischia. Off of Capri. He would take her there.

"Aren't you the dandy?" Mishka had mocked him, catching the look that passed between him and Alexandra. The young man from Kosovo turned away and tended to his own carryon. *He has to be jealous*, Roberto had thought. *Who wouldn't be?*

Mishka was dressed in casual travel clothes, while Stefan wore a herringbone blazer over brown dress-pants. They were tourists traveling in coach, while Alexandra would be joining Roberto in first class. Where he would endure the torture of pretending not to know her.

No matter. He would make up for it later.

"All right." Stefan had gathered them around a battered table. "You know what you're supposed to do. You all know your parts." He'd slowly turned his gray-blue eyes to each of them. "As of this moment, operation 'Independence' is under way."

Roberto arrived at the security checkpoint. Smoothly, he laid his bag down on the conveyor belt. He felt strangely calm. He was a businessman. He had a right to be there, just as Stefan had said.

"Any computers or recording equipment, please open them," sang out a harried attendant.

The security people looked exhausted and irritable, and well they should. Stefan had been ecstatic when word of the strike and subsequent work slowdown had hit the news. Over-burdened security people were less inclined to do a thorough job.

An overweight, middle-aged woman was sitting on a stool behind the monitor, and the security guard to her right was fussing with a stroller that had tangled with a garment bag coming through the conveyor.

Roberto knew that Stefan had said to keep to himself but... "Hello!" He offered the woman a barely accented greeting, quickly followed by a blazingly white smile. He could just imagine how good he looked: his muscled body clothed in a designer suit...the white of his teeth against his olive skin...his deeply-set green eyes capturing the frazzled security worker in an empathetic "tough day?" gaze.

"Hi," she said, pushing an errant lock of hair behind her ear. She cracked the slightest of smiles at him in return before looking back to her monitor. By then, his bag was already through. Without breaking his stride, he picked up his bag and moved off towards gate 22.

He was a businessman. He had a right to be there.

# Chapter 2

"So I thought I'd have a layover in Rome like you, Becky, but instead they assigned me to the 2260 back to New York. Can you believe that?" Trish Dugan looked to her colleagues for support, but Joan and Becky kept their heads down as they made their way to the gate. "I don't understand it. After all, you'd think my seniority would count for something."

"That's a bummer," Becky said half-heartedly. She felt badly for the woman; knew she'd been unhappy with her job for quite some time. And, by the looks of how Trish's uniform was fitting

her...differently, the Californian sur-
mised that she'd been eating her way
through her recent troubles. Still, the
thought of Trish complaining all the way
across the Atlantic was not appealing.
She would have her hands full already,
handling her passengers and trying to
stay out of the way of the mercurial Captain Phillips.

It happened quickly.

A surge of passengers was arriving
from a nearby gate, heading towards the
terminal. Their path was blocked by the
main flow of traffic moving towards the
outlying gates. There was a logjam
forming down-stream and disaster was
imminent.

"Ronny, over here, dear!" A mother
called to her young son. He had to be no
more than ten years old, and the mother
had evidently decided to let him 'enter-
tain' himself by dragging a small piece
of wheeled luggage on his own, as if it
were a pull-toy.

"Daddy's this way!" She yodeled,
motioning the boy after her. Unfortunately, that meant the child's path
swerved directly in front of the Orbis
flight attendants rushing in the opposite
direction. Somehow, Trish and Joan
stopped in time. But Becky, with her

head still down, didn't see the pull-strap and bag until it was too late.

Her knees and feet tangled in the strap, and Becky let go of her own pull-case as she felt her body pitch forward out of control.

"Aaah–!" She reached her hands out in front of her, bracing for impact, when suddenly two strong arms caught her from behind. She hung there, suspended in mid-air it seemed, until those same arms propped her back upright.

"What the..." she gasped. The air had rushed from her body when she'd begun to fall, leaving her breathless.

"Ronny, that wasn't very nice!" The luggage strap rested at Rebecca's feet, lying there like an uncoiled snake. The mother swiped it up with one hand and grabbed her son with the other. "Sorry!" she smiled, but her voice was insincere, and quickly she and Ronny melted back into the crowd.

"Are you okay?" A low voice sounded from above and behind her.

Becky spun around and looked up into the cool blue eyes of Captain 'Frosty' Phillips.

"I...uh...yeah, I think so," she said, flustered, smoothing her skirt.

"This yours?" The pilot maneuvered the handle of a wheeled flight bag to the younger woman's side.

"Yes...th—"

"See you on the flight deck..." blue eyes flickered down to Rebecca's nametag, "...Hanson." Then, after a quick nod to Joan Wetherill, she was gone.

Joan and Trish simply stood there, slack-jawed. Finally, the crew chief spoke, shaking her head in wonder. "Uh-oh. You're off to some start, Champ."

\* \* \* \* \* \* \* \* \* \*

It was done. She had surprised herself with the slight hesitation, as her hand hovered over the Orbis interoffice mail slot. She'd turned to stare out the floor-to-ceiling windows, watching the planes move slowly along the tarmac like great finned fish swimming in a gray concrete sea. And in those few seconds of deliberation, a thousand thoughts had stormed through her mind.

Was she doing the right thing? Was it as simple as running from Orbis to Federated Parcel, or was she running from something deeper, more profound, that she couldn't or wouldn't put her finger on? She hadn't been happy in a long time, she knew that much. It was easy enough to attribute those feelings to work. Therefore, in her highly analytical mind, a change in jobs should mean a change in outlook, right?

Cyrus Vandegrift, Colonel (Ret), USAF, now director of flight operations for Orbis, would be disappointed, she knew. Her old mentor had lured her to Orbis four years ago when he'd heard through the military grapevine what had happened. To Catherine Phillips, he was the father she'd never had. Or wished she had. She would make him see, in time, that it was for the best.

She returned her gaze to the letter in her hand, addressed to the grizzled Air Force veteran.

Yes, he would be angry. But she'd given her decision plenty of thought, she rationalized.

For hours, during her down time, she had stared at the antiseptic white walls of her Manhattan apartment, sparsely decorated lest she ever begin to think of it as someplace permanent. A home. She had paced the floor, wearing a hole in the carpet and gazed out over the city. She'd watched the people and cars spinning and turning like ducks in a shooting gallery, and wondered what the secret of it all was. Were they happy? What key to life did they have that she didn't? And she had thought about another time, another place, when she'd quit. For something better, or so she had hoped then.

She held none of those illusions now.

The Federated job would be different, nothing more.

With a sigh, she had released the letter and watched it flutter into the bin.

The pilot hadn't gone far when she had anticipated the accident about to happen between that kid and the flight attendant. It had all seemed so clear to her as it unfolded, like blipping targets on a flight simulator screen: 'A + B = Crash.'

She didn't know how she covered the ground to the young woman so quickly; she was only relieved to see that the girl hadn't hurt herself.

Rebecca Hanson.

She'd seen her name on the crew list, and though she had never flown with her before, she understood from quiet comments here and there that the girl was well respected—a real comer. She had to be, or she wouldn't have pulled such a preferred flight route in the first place.

The taller woman was amused to see the fearful look on Hanson's face after she'd caught her in mid-fall. What – did she think she would bite her or something? Maybe so...she had to have heard some of the stories about her, at least. People talked.

Well, last trip out or not, if this 'Hanson' couldn't pull her weight, Catherine Phillips would let her know about it.

Kate left the stunned flight attendants behind as she strode towards the gate. Attempting to focus her concentration on the upcoming flight, as was her habit, the pilot found herself slightly annoyed at a puzzle that kept tugging at her memory. There was something about that young blonde that was so...familiar. But she hadn't crewed with her before, Kate was certain. No, she would have remembered her.

* * * * * * * * * *

"Hi!"

"Welcome aboard!"

"Here, let me help you with that...."

An unending stream of passengers flowed down the jetway ramp, bottle-necking as usual at the entrance to the main cabin. Nathan and Cindy played traffic cops, directing people fore and aft, while Joan and Becky were already providing pre-flight service to the first and business class passengers. Alan and Trish assumed duties in the rear galley, making sure that the foodstuffs required for the long flight were present and accounted for. The one thing worse than cranky, tired passengers were cranky, tired, *hungry* passengers.

The Boeing 777-200 was a big plane, one of the largest in Orbis' flight service, and for this particular route, the airline had fitted it out for three classes: first class, business, and coach. All told, the aircraft could carry just over 300 passengers, the bulk of whom – nearly 230 – would be economy class. The crew complement for a full flight should have been at least six for the main cabin, as well as another two or three for business and first class. Joan Wetherill and her team would be stretched to the limit for this flight.

"This is ridiculous!" Trish Dugan muttered, watching the rows of coach seats—two seats on either side and five seats across the middle—fill up. "I'm going to make sure the union hears about this!"

Alan Ross said nothing, merely rolling his blue eyes in response. Trish was right—it would be a rough flight being so short-staffed, but complaining about it wouldn't help matters any. He turned his eyes down the main cabin, where once in a while he could catch the blonde head of Becky Hanson as she cheerfully went about her duties. Funny. The additional workload hadn't seemed to bother the young Californian. From the moment they'd stepped aboard, Becky had simply set to it. She accepted the hardship and moved on. It was one of the things Alan admired about her, and he smiled to himself at that thought.

"Alan, it looks like 32C is having trouble with that stroller," Trish said, making no move to help out.

"Got it," Alan sighed, and he wedged himself down the crowded aisle towards a harried mother and toddler. The last thing he wanted was to have Trish Dugan bitching in his ear all the way to Rome. Worse, he would be stuck in the tube with her on the 2260 return flight tomorrow. Great.

"Here ma'am, let me help you with that." Alan reached for the offending stroller. The mother gratefully stepped aside, letting the handsome flight attendant take charge. So engrossed was Alan in properly stowing the awkwardly shaped stroller, that he took little notice of the black-haired tourist type sitting two rows back. He wore a herringbone jacket, and he stared right through Alan with his icy, gray-blue eyes. The flight attendant was too preoccupied with the stroller to take notice. After all, the man was simply another passenger. He had a right to be there.

\* \* \* \* \* \* \* \* \*

Catherine Phillips had already been aboard for some time, choosing to punch her access code into the jetway keypad as soon as she had arrived at the gate. She normally enjoyed being first aboard the aircraft, her aircraft, and although the end of the line was near, today was no exception.

Using the service door, she had quickly slipped out of the plane and performed her "walk around," taking little notice of the late afternoon chill. She walked the length of the sleek airframe,

visually confirming the tell-tale droop of
the starboard wing as jet fuel was
pumped into the tankage; she laid a hand
on the side of the port six-wheeled bogie
the big plane sported on its undercarriage.  At last she peeked through the
nacelles of the twin jet engines, catching
sight of the great turbofans concealed
within them.  Satisfied with what she
saw, she climbed back aboard.

Kate chose to ignore the bustle of
the ground service crew in the cabin
behind her as they cleaned and restocked
the plane for the overseas flight.  Passing by the workers, the pilot had taken
off her cap and slipped out of her coat
and jacket, stowing them in the small
crew valet just outside the cockpit.

Closing the door behind her, she
ducked onto the flight deck, sweeping
her eyes along the large dual-control
instrumentation array, fully digitalized
onboard the big 777-200.  She paused for
a moment, taking it all in.  Then quietly,
with a faint whisper of a sound, she
eased herself into the leather pilot's seat.
Bill Samuelson, her first officer on this
flight, hadn't arrived yet, and that was
fine with Kate.

This was her time, when she men-
tally went through her pre-flight check,

and she wistfully recalled days past
when even the simple anticipation of
every new flight left her breathless. It
had been some time since she'd felt that
way.

She did not put on her headphones
yet, choosing instead to absorb the
sounds and sensations of the plane; it
was as if it lived and breathed all around
her, as if she were in the belly of a beast.
The soft hiss of the air through the
inflow vents. The muffled thumps from
the refueling team. The vibrations of the
wing tanks through the fuselage as the
plane thirstily drank in the jet fuel. The
groans and bangs from the cargo bays as
the luggage was stowed.

Oftentimes she had wondered
whether the secret to a successful mission, to a good flight, was allowing herself to become a fully mechanized,
computerized, automaton—to become
one with the plane. Or, was it in breathing a spark of sentient life into the two
hundred fifty tons of fully loaded steel
alloy she rode on nearly every
day...joining in an unholy communion
with the beast and taming it under the
firm guidance of her hand? Cyrus
Vandegrift was bound to have an opinion

or two about that, and she smiled to herself at the thought.

The door at the far end of the jetway burst open, and she heard the pounding of footsteps hurrying along the ramp. She opened her eyes just as the chatter of the flight crew behind her signaled their arrival onboard.

And an end to her meditations.

It would be a rough flight, being so short-staffed, but if anyone could make the best of it, the pilot thought Joan Wetherill and her crew could. As long as the new girl didn't muck things up too badly.

"Captain!" Bill Samuelson poked his salt and pepper head inside the cockpit. Samuelson was a commercial pilot all the way. He'd worked himself up through the ranks from flight school to small planes, logging his hours, advancing to mid-sized jets and now the big birds. Kate had never said so, but she admired the man's initiative and drive.

Bill was her senior in terms of age, but her junior in terms of rank, and he always was mindful of that whenever they worked together. He followed her orders, was supportive, reliable, and had a steady hand. Kate couldn't ask for more from any first officer.

"Hi, Bill." She casually waved a hand in greeting. "How's it look?"

"We've got a full boat," the older man said, sliding into the seat at Kate's right, and reaching for his headset. "If we're lucky, the chicken kiev will knock 'em out once we're under way!" He grinned at the dark-haired pilot.

Kate could not help it—she returned her first officer's smile with a small one of her own. Quickly, she chose to refocus her attention on the tasks at hand, donning her own headset and checking a printout of the weather update. Once they got above the cloud deck, it looked like smooth sailing all the way from JFK to Leonardo da Vinci airport. Or, 'Fiumicino', as the Italians called it.

Good. The passengers might sleep after all.

At her side, Bill had pressed a command on his touch-sensitive control panel, initiating the electronic display of the 777-200's pre-flight checklist. "Ready when you are, Captain." He paused, waiting for her command.

"Okay, let's fire this bird up," Kate said, keying in the ignition sequence, pressing the final switch with her thumb. The Pratt & Whitney 4098 engines, each bigger than the average compact car, rumbled to life.

Kate heard Bill's calm voice through her headset methodically calling off the points on the checklist. They worked in tandem, smoothly and professionally, prepping the plane for departure. Soon, they would be under way.

And for Catherine Phillips, there would be no turning back.

\* \* \* \* \* \* \* \* \* \*

It was happening; after all the planning, they were actually doing it! Roberto Andizzi watched Alexandra Sadrio take the seat just behind his own. She had moved through the first class cabin as if she had never seen him before, and though he tried to avert his gaze as Stefan had told him he should, he couldn't help but steal a glimpse of her as she passed by. After all, he had a right to look, didn't he? He, a wealthy, attractive businessman, admiring a beautiful woman – his woman – as she took her seat.

Roberto had seen Stefan and Mishka earlier in the throng of passengers swarming at the gate; so they too had successfully made it through the besieged security checkpoints! But as a first class passenger, he had boarded ahead of them both. He hadn't seen Alexandra at all and he had worried for her, until at last he saw her tall, blonde form fill the entrance to the cabin. Now he could relax, at least until they were under way. Until the signal was given.

"Wait for it," Stefan had said. And how many times they had rehearsed it! To assure themselves—Stefan most of all—that there would be no failure.

At times, Stefan's resolve had irritated Roberto. After all, he was only doing this for the money—and for his Alex. But for Stefan, Alex, and Mishka, this was about their homeland—their people. Roberto did not understand much of it, but he understood well enough the anger that flashed through Stefan's dead eyes whenever the purpose of their mission was discussed: to bring the Americans fully into the fight for freedom and independence in Kosovo, to force out the hated Serbian butchers and give the ethnic Albanians a homeland to call their own.

The time for negotiation and compromise was over, Stefan had sworn to them. He would bring the eyes of the world down upon the Americans and force their hand. To hell with NATO and their worthless talk, treaties, and impotent bombing runs. In the end, it all had merely rained more suffering down upon his people. He would force the indecisive Americans to drive the Serbs from the Kosovars' rightful homeland, one kilometer at a time.

Independence—denied them so far by the Yugoslavs and NATO—would bring peace to Kosovo. Stefan was sure of it.

And for now, Stefan was willing to use any and all means at his disposal to reach that end. Roberto's maternal grandfather had been born in Albania and had migrated across the Adriatic to Italy many years ago—Stefan routinely reminded the Italian military pilot of that fact. Still, this was not his fight. It was too much to risk, had it not been for Alexandra. How lucky he was that the beauty had come into his life, and he would do anything to keep her a part of it—even this.

"I'll take a Campari and soda," he heard himself saying to the attractive, shorthaired flight attendant who had suddenly appeared at his side. "With just a little ice." He winked at her sea-green eyes.

"I can handle that!" She smiled at him, and he found himself watching the sway of her hips in her tight blue skirt as she turned and moved off towards the galley. She was teasing him; he knew it! *Anyway, it wouldn't hurt to pass the time flirting with the little blonde*, he thought. *It was what any Italian businessman would do, wasn't it?* And it didn't hurt that Alexandra would be left to seethe behind him, in silence. After all, a little jealousy was good for a relationship, his father had taught him that.

Alex would be angry with him afterwards, or so he hoped. She was beautiful when she was angry.

*********

For the fourth time, Mishka Rhu checked that his seat belt was fastened low and tight across his lap. He didn't like to fly. In fact, he'd rarely flown at all, given the life he'd led back in Pristina as a technical engineering graduate student at the university. But the war, Stefan, and the death of his little sister, Natasha—shot and killed while walking home from school with several of her friends—had changed all that.

The grief of his parents over the loss of their daughter had continued to deepen, like a worsening cancer. She was gone forever, as were the memories of the peaceful, happy times of their life together as a family. His father had turned to drink, his mother to her bed, and Mishka to the KLA—the Kosovo Liberation Army—as the means of easing the despair in their respective lives.

Mishka had committed himself to the hit-and-run, house-to-house guerrilla style warfare that the KLA favored against their Serbian oppressors, but as months passed and still nothing had changed, he'd grown more and more disillusioned. Even NATO was only willing to go so far, supporting the Kosovars in their quest for peace and self-rule, but not in the independence from Serbia that would guarantee the peace for future generations.

Mishka had heard the stories from his parents and grandparents; he knew what the Serbs were capable of. And hadn't they shown this to the world already? Independence was the only answer. Only freedom would pay a final homage to the sacrifice of Natasha and the others, the untold thousands of victims of the invaders.

But Stefan Bukoshi, the passionate man with a cool exterior who lurked around the coffee houses frequented by the KLA student sympathizers, seemed to have an answer. His intense, deep-set eyes, his high cheekbones, and long, slim face drew them all into his rebel rhetoric. And it didn't hurt that the beautiful Alexandra was never far from his side. It wasn't until after Stefan had taken him and several of his KLA cell members into his confidence, that he realized she belonged to the irritating Italian pilot Bukoshi had recruited into his plan.

That pompous fly-boy fool!

"My name is Joan, I'll be your first flight attendant this evening on Orbis flight #2240, flying non-stop to Rome. May I please direct your attention to our safety video…"

Mishka swallowed hard and pushed himself back into his seat as his personal video unit displayed the emergency procedures.

"Please be sure all electronic devices, including computers, cell phones, and radios, are switched off until ten minutes after take-off…"

Mishka could feel the sweat beading on his forehead. He knew Stefan sat several rows behind him, but he dared not turn around. He knew he was doing the right thing; he was sure of it. It was just that this damned airplane was making him so nervous, not that he'd ever give that Italian asshole up in first class the satisfaction of ever letting him know it.

"There are six exit doors on the Boeing 777-200..."

He concentrated on his breathing.

"Keep in mind the nearest exit may be behind you..."

Mishka had already counted the rows.

"In the event of a water landing..."

*In the event of a water landing!* Mishka squeezed his eyes shut and tried not to visualize the plane plummeting into the sea. *Oh God, I can't swim!*

\* \* \* \* \* \* \* \* \* \*

*"Flight attendants, prepare for departure."* The smooth voice of first officer, Bill Samuelson, filtered through the intercom.

Cindy Walters and Nathan Berbick performed one last visual check of the main cabin, working their way back to the aft jump seats where Trish Dugan and Alan Ross had already strapped themselves in.

Nathan moved along quickly, that last coffee in the airport having done wonders to clear his hangover. He tapped the tops of each seat back as he passed, checking that they were in the upright position. The darkly attractive young man looked over at Cindy, working her way down the opposite aisle. As usual, he would finish before her.

Cindy always seemed to take extra time chatting unnecessarily with the passengers. Hell, she was doing it even now! Nathan smiled in spite of himself as he went by her. That Southern belle of his. She surely loved to talk. A perfect counterbalance to his moody silences, he knew. He could never stay angry long, not with her around. *So, she's giving me another chance in Rome. That's all I need,* he thought.

"Sir, could you make sure your bag is fully under the seat in front of you?" The Charleston accent in the voice was clear and strong.

He would not panic. He was cool. He was calm. He, the leader of "Operation Independence." "Certainly," Stefan Bukoshi replied in formal English, pushing his carryon under the seat. He turned his gray-blue eyes to the petite, brunette flight attendant, and offered her a thin-lipped smile.

"Thank you," she said, returning the smile, and she moved on, looking past him.

"You're welcome," he said softly, turning to gaze out the window at a gun-metal sky.

\* \* \* \* \* \* \* \* \* \*

"I think you've got a fan in 2C," Joan laughed, sitting down next to Becky in a forward jump seat.

"Please," Becky held up her palm in protest. "As long as he's not like that guy on the JFK to LAX run," and she shook her head, remembering.

"I don't know," the older woman tightened her seat belt, "he's not that bad looking."

"Exactly. I'll bet there's not a beautiful woman—or mirror—he passes by. No thanks. Not my type."

"Good thing Cindy's not working first class," Joan said, chuckling. "If Nathan ever got a load of 'Mr. GQ', he'd have a hissy-fit of monumental proportions."

"Been there, seen that," Becky
shared a knowing look with the senior
flight attendant. Nathan and Cindy were
her friends, but when they got together,
it could be explosive at times. She fell
silent for a moment, considering how she
might take a rain check on hanging with
them during the Rome layover. She'd
been thinking anyway how it might be
more fun to strike out exploring on her
own and leave the lovebirds elsewhere in
the Eternal City. *Not a bad idea at that*,
she resolved.

There was a slight bump as the plane
taxied to a stop, waiting its turn in the
take-off queue. Bill Samuelson had
already announced that they were fourth
in line, so it wouldn't be long now.
Becky had thought it strange how the
first officer was handling all communi-
cation from the flight deck, but Joan had
told her earlier that this was not unusual
when crewing with Captain Phillips.
The pilot preferred to delegate such
tasks to her first officer, concentrating
on flying instead.

And Kate Phillips was a serious one;
that was for sure. Joan had taken a
moment to formally introduce the young
flight attendant to the captain, shortly
after they'd come aboard. After knock-

ing, Joan had boldly entered the spacious flight deck, while Becky barely dared to poke her head in.

"Hiya there, Becky!" Bill Samuelson had removed his headphones and grabbed one of her hands in both of his, shaking it heartily. Becky knew the older man and liked him; she'd flown with him a number of times and found him to be warm and engaging. He was quick to laugh, and it was a running joke between them how he slyly kept offering to fix her up with his son, the doctor.

"Captain, this is Rebecca Hanson." Joan gestured toward the small blonde.

The pilot barely turned her head, giving the two women a quick nod. But it was enough for Becky to once again feel as though she'd been run through by the sidelong look. What was it about that woman's gaze that made her feel so awkward?

"Hanson." The captain returned her attention to the active matrix cockpit displays. "Welcome aboard."

"Thanks," Becky had finally choked out, beating a hasty retreat back through the doorway. *I think...*she added silently to herself. *Only 4,300 miles to Rome!*

\*\*\*\*\*\*\*\*\*\*

Captain Catherine Phillips found herself looking up the butt-end of a United Airlines 737. They were just that one plane away from being cleared for take-off. Kate heard the tower direct the UAL plane onto the runway, and she found herself gazing fondly at an aircraft that was truly the workhorse of the skies. She'd flown the efficiently designed 737 more times than she cared to recall. A big jet in its day, it was dwarfed by the Orbis Airlines 777-200 that trailed behind it now.

When Kate had first started flying the 777 super-jets, she was amazed at how the avionics of the aircraft had so closely resembled what she'd been used to in the Air Force: state of the art flight management, flat panel displays, and satellite-based navigation, all utilizing fully integrated fiber-optic technology.

Many pilots, Kate Phillips included, thought that the most impressive feature of the 777 line was its 'fly by wire' or 'FBW' flight director system. The European AirBuses were the first commercial carriers to utilize this revolutionary digital flight manager. In conventional aircraft, flight control surfaces such as flaps and ailerons were mechanically linked to the control column on the flight deck. But on the 777, control surfaces were now moved by computers that interpreted the pilot's commands.

The triple-redundant system replaced heavy cables, complicated pulleys, and brackets with a wire designed to electrically transmit signals to the flying surfaces. Aircraft instability, linked to flaws in the automatic pilot system, had become virtually a non-factor.

Kate stared at her control column. If she were to pull up on it, the computer would sense that she wanted the aircraft to climb. The computer would then activate the flight control surfaces—increasing the camber of the ailerons on the wings, raising the tail elevators—to comply with that command. The damn thing was so good, Kate wondered at times whether a pilot was even needed.

The Federated Parcel planes were not equipped with FBW systems, and a part of Kate was glad of it. Truth be known, she preferred 'hands-on' flying.

"Orbis two-two-four-zero, taxi to the leading edge of runway three-five-alpha and hold short."

"Roger, Orbis two-two-four-zero." Kate acknowledged the control tower over the din of the United 737 roaring past. They were one plane away from take-off.

Next to her, Bill pulled the throttle out to idle power and continued reviewing the pre-flight checklist. "Be nice to get out of this cold," he said in an aside.

"Mmmm..." Kate's voice was non-committal. She would miss working with Bill, though she doubted he would feel the same. But that was her problem, wasn't it...that she still gave a damn what people thought.

"Kennedy tower to Orbis two-two-four-zero, you are cleared for take-off on three-five-alpha."

Kate taxied the plane to the top of the runway, and the twin PW4098's gunned to a feverish whine. "Roger, wilco Kennedy tower. Orbis two-two-four-zero at runway three-five-alpha, ready for takeoff." She flashed Bill a quick look. "Full throttle," she ordered, and the jet began to accelerate down the runway.

The display panels came alive, shouting their bits of information at the pilot: airspeed, wind, heading, engine temperature and rpms. Kate felt a flare of excitement in her belly; she always did at take-off. It was in her blood after all, she supposed. She watched the speed display leap forward: 75, 150, 200 mph, as Bill called it out. She pressed forward on the elevator trim and felt her co-pilot's warm hand beneath her own, backing her up. It wasn't really necessary, not with the FBW, but it showed that her first officer was a pilot of the old school: procedures and routine first, and the younger woman appreciated that.

*There!* It was time. Kate's gut would've told her so, even if the digital displays hadn't already.

Lift-off.

She pulled back on the control column, and the plane responded. The nose began to rise up gently, and instantly she vectored in on her optimal rate and level of climb, banking to the west and into a head wind as she did so.

"Wheels up."

"Roger, wheels up," Samuelson confirmed, and Kate could tell he was right by the hydraulic hum of the nose wheel and twin bogies as they retracted into the airframe.

The 95,000 pounds of thrust generated by the jet engines pressed the pilot hard into her seat, and she knew that the passengers and crew behind her were feeling that same stirring power; at once

frightening,    impressive—and    highly
effective.

Higher and higher the plane climbed,
occasionally    buffeted    by    the    storm
clouds they passed through, the same
snowy system that had plagued New
York all weekend. In the main cabin, the
passengers were silent as the overhead
bins rattled and the seat backs shook
with the force of the engine burst.
Finally, at about 12,000 feet, they
punched through the cloud deck and into
one of the most beautiful sunsets Kate
thought she had ever seen—and she'd
seen plenty here above the clouds.

"Wow," Bill said. "Neat."

Kate    smiled    faintly    at    her    first
officer's understatement. "Turning on a
heading of one-one-zero."

"One-one-zero,    roger    that,"    Bill
replied, as Kate began to fly the plane
towards the east; climbing all the while,
with a vertical speed of over 2500 feet
per minute. Soon, they would be at their
cruising altitude of 33,000 feet.

The pilot could not help but admire
the view as they strained skyward. The
sun had already slipped away, and as far
as she could see, the western horizon
glowed as though it were aflame, like a
fire on a desert plain. Hot, red embers at

the base of it bled into singed amber, finally topped off with the cooling topaz of the descending darkness.

Yes, she'd seen sunsets before, but this one touched her in a way that surprised her. Her mind briefly skipped back to the berry-flavored Popsicle of her youth, with a trio of colors like this sunset, the kind her father had brought her on those sweltering hot summer afternoons at Coney Island.

How tall and dark her father had seemed next to her as they strolled along, her little hand held up safely in the grasp of his beefy palm. One brother was too little to come with them, while her older one didn't care to, and that was fine with her. She loved having her handsome father all to herself.

Together, they would walk the fair grounds, watching the other kids on the tilt-a-whirl; on the scrambler.

"Please, Poppa, take me on the roller coaster!" she would beg. High and fast. Even then she craved it.

"Not this time, Katie," he'd say, a hint of sadness in his voice, and he would ruffle the dark hair—so much like his own—on the top of her head.

It wasn't until much later that she realized he couldn't afford to pay for all those rides like the other kids' dads could. And by then he'd been long dead.

Catherine Phillips' father would never live to be a rich man. Not on what little money he cleared from the tiny Greek storefront he owned in Queens. The small business was all the legacy he had from his own father, an immigrant from Greece who passed through Ellis Island in 1923 in search of a better life. He left behind everything he had in the land of his birth, forsaking all for this new land of opportunity.

And somewhere as he passed through those gates of promise, with the Statue of Liberty gazing down sublimely upon him, keeping her secrets to herself, he left behind the "i" at the end of his name. Most likely, thanks to a harried customs-house bookkeeper's error, Stavros Philippi became Stavros Phillips.

It was just as well for the wide-eyed 17-year-old from the Peloponnese. It meant he belonged. He was a poor farmer's son, but his children would be Americans. And his children's children. His joy knew no bounds, though it was short-lived.

Stavros didn't travel far. He settled in Queens, in a fine Greek neighborhood

off 35th street, and he tried to build a
life for himself, his new wife, and a
growing brood of children.

He served the foodstuffs of Greece
to his homesick fellow immigrants: the
fish, the feta cheese, the lamb. It was a
hard life made harder still by the poor
health of his fair wife. She died all too
young, from a cough that wouldn't leave
her, despite all the tonics that quack of a
doctor sold him.

Stavros never stopped mourning for
the wife he lost, and for the children who
left him one by one, seeking better for-
tunes across the river. They headed
west, into the heart of the big city and
beyond. Time passed and he heard little
from them as they built their lives elsewhere, and so he was overjoyed when
his youngest son—Nicholas—announced
that he was interested in making a go of
the family business.

It did not matter that Nicholas had
courted and wed a tall, redheaded Irish
girl. Stavros had recognized soon
enough that the new Mrs. Meghan Phillips had a backbone of iron and a blazing
temperament to accompany it. She
would do well, helping her husband in
the business and bearing fine young sons

besides! It was a love match between those two. Stavros could see it.

And so, at peace with this small bit of happiness in his heart, Stavros Phillips, adopted son of America, went to sleep one warm spring night in 1970 and did not wake up.

Nicholas and Meghan barely had time to mourn, as busy as they were with "The Olympia"—so Nicholas had named their emporium—and their small children. Peter, the oldest, sported the same red locks as his mother; then came Catherine, a raven-haired, blue-eyed firebrand that Nicholas had delighted in, and finally Brendan, the fair, tow-headed baby of the family.

It may have been decided for her that Meghan Phillips would help to run a Greek fish-house in Queens, but by God if it was the last thing she did, she had sworn to the Blessed Virgin Mary and to herself that her children would all have proper Irish names. Knowing this was a fight he was destined to lose, Nicholas had capitulated to his bride's wishes. In this matter, anyway.

A child can tell when she is the apple of a parent's eye, and so it was with Katie and Nicholas. For as much time as the boys spent with their mother, little Kate did with her father. And those rare, infrequent sojourns to Coney Island, alone with her Poppa, were what she treasured most.

She would never know what caused her father to put a bullet through his brain when she was only 12. Her mother never talked about it. And Kate had always been too hurt, too angry, to ask. She thought she would never live to know such a terrible heartache again, to feel such a loss, and indeed that was so, at least until Brendan had been killed.

Catherine Phillips sighed. The western horizon began to fade away behind her, a silent elegy to a promise unfulfilled, as the plane banked towards the darkened east. Towards Rome.

*Shake it off, woman! What the hell's the matter with you?* The pilot self-consciously cleared her throat and straightened up a bit in her seat. Something had set her off. Perhaps the knowledge that a part of her life was coming to an end. Changing. Or maybe it was the disappointment she knew she would hear in Cyrus' voice, made all the more biting because in her own heart she feared she would feel the same way. Or perhaps it was the fair-haired looks of that new flight attendant, Rebecca Hanson. Not

only her coloring, but her manner too—
shy yet confident—reminded Kate of the
brother she'd lost. Not that it mattered.

*None of this matters,* Kate thought,
as the plane struck out high above the
Atlantic, sweeping eastward over darkened, turbulent waters. *It never did.*

# Chapter
# 3

"Got any more chicken kiev up here, hon?" Cindy Walters brushed back a stray wisp of brunette hair from her forehead. "There's a rush on it in coach."

"Well..." Becky turned towards the mini-oven in the forward galley, her brow furrowed. "...I've got three or four more in this last batch, but that's it."

"Go figure, huh?" Alan Ross pressed his tall form into the galley space alongside the two women. Even on such a large aircraft as the 777-200, the galleys were little more than walk-in closets.

"Alan, what are you doing up here?" Becky spun towards a now-beeping oven.

"Chicken kiev hunting, what else?" his white teeth flashed from his tan face.

The young flight attendant shook her head. "And you left Trish back there all alone?"

Rebecca Hanson might not have been a senior flight attendant yet, but she had a natural instinct for organization and leadership. Her peers recognized her ability and responded to it well. It was one of the reasons why she'd moved up so quickly through the Orbis ranks in the first place.

"Hah. You don't think she'd actually want to get off her butt and come up here herself, do you, Champ?"

"Alan..."

"She's not alone, Becky," Cindy starting picking through the wrapped dinners that Becky had begun extracting from the oven. "Nathan is with her." She paused and then turned to her friends with a stricken look. "Oh God...what did I just say?"

"Ow!" Becky accidentally touched a loose foil wrap—oven hot. "Darn it!" She quickly whipped her index finger to her mouth.

"Here, let me do that for you," Alan volunteered, reaching for her hand instead of the dinners.

*Thwack!*  Becky swatted his hand away.  She shoved two chicken kievs in his chest and began propelling him backwards, out of the galley.

"Here.  Go!"

"B–but–"

"Get back there.  Now!  Before Trish and Nathan kill each other!"

"No fair, Becky, I was here first!"  Cindy cast an accusing eye at Alan's retreating back.

"I know," Rebecca said, belatedly pulling on an oven mitt.  "Let me make it up to you.  I can give you one more chicken..."  She retrieved the last of the dinners from the oven, and began arranging them on her roller cart.  "...and how about a couple of these filets from first class?  And I won't even talk about the manicotti."

"Who loves ya, darlin'?"  Cindy reached for the proffered meals and twirled out of the galley with a wave.

The first class curtain parted and Joan Wetherill entered from the opposite side, just in time to see the Southerner leaving.

"Problem?"

"No," Becky grinned. "None at all."

\* \* \* \* \* \* \* \* \*

"I'm telling you, Nathan, it was *A Bug's Life.*"

"Antz."

"A Bug's Life!"

*"ANTZ!"* The young man's closely cropped dark head was barely visible as he probed a low storage cabinet, virtually crawling into it on his hands and knees.

"You're wrong." Trish slouched against the counter, crossing her arms in front of her chest.

"*Whatever.*" Nathan Berbick swiveled his head around to glare balefully over his shoulder at his colleague. "I don't see *you* helping to find it!"

"C'mon you guys." Alan rolled a food cart loaded with discarded dinner trays into the aft galley. "We can't watch *CNN Highlights* from here to the continent." He looked from Trish to Nathan's half-hidden form, and back again. "Can we?"

"GOT it!" Nathan backed out of the darkened cubby, waving a video cassette case.

The blonde surfer plucked the tape from his hand. "YES" he crowed. "I LOVE this movie!"

"*A Bug's Life?*" Trish's skepticism was plain.

Nathan stood, brushing speckles of dirt from his knees. "Nah—*Antz*—right buddy?" and he clapped Alan on the back.

"What?" Alan looked up from the cassette, confusion written on his face. "No way. *Star Trek: Insurrection!*" and he handed the case to Trish. "Check this out!" He stepped away from the cart, and dropped his arms outward from his waist as if he were holding an invisible 'Mac-10' automatic rifle. "Lock and load!" he intoned, in an overly dramatic voice that more resembled Jack Nicholson than Mr. Data.

The dark cloud of pique lifted from Nathan, and he laughed aloud at his friend's attempt at humor.

Trish Dugan found not a thing funny about the matter. And if she thought for one minute that these two clowns might be ahead of her on Orbis' promotion track...well...she'd slit her wrists right here and now!

"Ugh!" she slapped the tape into the player, turning her back on the men's guffaws.  "Load *this!*"

\* \* \* \* \* \* \* \* \* \*

Joan Wetherill rolled a half-empty serving cart back into the fore galley and stepped on the toe brake.  "That covers us through 12," she said, indicating that all the first and business class passengers had been attended to.  "Can you finish up here, Becky?"  The senior flight attendant wiped her hands off on a towel.  "I'm going to help them clear back in coach.  Show's about to start!"

"No problem," Becky replied.

"Oh," the older woman paused before heading out, "could you take care of the captain?  Filet mignon.  I've already gotten a manicotti to Bill—he should be finishing up now."  Without waiting for a response, she whisked away.

"Uhh..." Becky scanned the remaining entrees in the cart, dreading the worst.  "Chicken...chicken...pasta..." she spoke softly to herself as she searched.  But it was no good.  There was not a filet to be found.

*Great,* she thought, straightening. And it was her own damn fault, too, for giving up those extras. With pasta and the infamous chicken kiev in hand, Becky took a deep breath and knocked firmly on the cockpit door.

"Hiya, Becky!" The smiling brown eyes of Bill Samuelson were instantly in front of her. "How's my favorite daughter-in-law?" he stepped back and ushered her onto the roomy flight deck.

"I wonder what Jimmy's wife would think of that?" Becky grinned, referring to Samuelson's other—very married—grown son. She unfolded a tray on one of two seats at the rear of the cockpit, designed for extra pilots on longer, trans-Pacific hauls. Many pilots preferred to relax over a meal there, rather than at the main control column. It helped to break up the monotony of an extended flight, where it was hard enough to dodge complacency on the new breed of highly automated jets. The captain still had her headphones on, intently looking out the front cockpit window into the nothingness of the dark.

Becky set the entrées down on top of the tray, and turned to clear the first officer's dinner from the adjacent seat. Bill had obviously enjoyed his manicotti, Becky thought, looking at the empty plate. As she removed his platter, she could not resist sparing a quick glance towards Flight 2240's pilot.

Catherine Phillips was just removing her headset, as her co-pilot slipped into the seat beside her. "Bon appetit," he said, scanning the flat panel displays of the flight director system. "I highly recommend the manicotti!"

Kate reached her arms above her head, stretching. "Not for me," she replied. "Filet all the way."

"Aaah—"

Kate turned and rested her eyes on Becky, as if noticing for the first time that the young flight attendant was even in the cockpit. "Hanson," she said noncommittally, moving towards the rear seat.

*Oh God, here it comes,* Becky worried. *She's gonna nail me.* "I'm sorry, Captain, b–but..."

The tall, slim pilot sat down, flicking her head slightly so that the plait of her luminous ebony hair rested on her back. She studied the two entrées on her tray, fingering them both.

"I said I wanted filet."

"I know but..." Becky panicked, and it all came tumbling out in a nervous burst. "You see, they were short of chicken in the main cabin, and so Cindy came up to first class looking for more. I was going to give her some, but then Alan...he needed a couple, too..."

Becky could feel the flame of embarrassment on her cheeks as the captain lifted a pair of piercing blue eyes to her own, taking in her pointless story. But Rebecca Hanson felt herself continue to tumble off balance in the presence of this woman, as surely as if she'd been tripped up once more by that kid's luggage strap.

To her own uniquely painful horror, she heard her voice blathering on. "So even though Cindy had been there first, I gave the chicken to Alan, and made up for it by giving Cindy the filets—I just wanted them to get back since we were so short-handed..."

"Yeesss..." The pilot's eyes narrowed.

Becky gulped. *This is it. I am doomed.* "So, I'm sorry, but there's no filet mignon left." Becky tried to muster some sense of professionalism in the face of the dark woman's stare. She tilted her chin up, waiting for the ax to fall. "Would you like the chicken kiev or the manicotti?" She concluded, using her best, brightest, flight attendant's voice.

"I'd take the manicotti, if I were you!" Bill Samuelson laughed from the front of the flight deck.

"Are the passengers all taken care of?"

"What?" Becky was temporarily flummoxed by the captain's question.

"The passengers—have they all eaten? Been served what they wanted?"

"Uh...YES!" Rebecca responded enthusiastically. At least the pilot could not fault her on that score. "Joan confirmed that the serving was completed."

"Good, that's all I care about," Kate Phillips eased back into her seat. "I'll take the chicken, Hanson."

"Don't say I didn't warn you!" Samuelson turned and winked at the two women over his shoulder, before returning his attention to the autopilot readings.

"Chicken it is," Becky said, relief flooding through her. She'd survived her first encounter with the notorious Captain 'Frosty.' And it hadn't been so bad after all. Concerned only for her passengers, the captain had understood and hadn't taken it out on her. Heck, maybe she could even grow to like this woman.   *Wouldn't that be a hoot?* she thought.

"Here," the pilot reached for the rejected manicotti entrée.

Becky balanced Bill Samuelson's discarded tray on one arm, while also quickly reaching for the manicotti with her free hand.  She intended on beating a very hasty retreat while she was ahead of the game.  Wait until she told Nathan how she thought the captain wasn't so terrible after all!  "No, let me—"

In an instant, disaster struck: Kate Phillips, reaching to lift the manicotti up, and Becky Hanson, bent at the knees and slightly off balance, reaching down to make a one-handed grab for the tray at the same time.

At the last minute, Becky tried to jerk her hand away, but she succeeded only in hitting the underside of the tray as if it were a seesaw.  In slow motion, Becky saw the platter flip, executing a perfect 180 degree turn, coming in for landing face down upon the pilot's lap.

A strange, strangled cry issued from Becky's throat, and she felt herself going weak in the knees.  She was frozen, unable to move, watching the red sauce and ricotta cheese ooze down the woman's right knee and onto the deck.

At last, she forced herself to raise her eyes to the pilot's face. How dark her features seemed now, and how high and fine her cheekbones were, Becky thought, as she took in the tight bunching and clenching of the jaw muscles. *She's pissed, all right,* Becky despaired, *and it's all my fault.*

Slowly, the pilot swiveled to face her. She picked up a segment of rolled pasta, and calmly deposited it on her plate, next to a piece of chicken. "This," her steel-blue eyes knifed through the young blonde, "is not good."

\* \* \* \* \* \* \* \* \* \*

The opening credits to the in-flight movie had just begun to roll, when Stefan Bukoshi smoothly reached under the seat in front of him, tugging out his carry-on. In the darkened interior of the cabin, he could see Mishka seated several rows ahead, stock-still. They were on a timetable and, though Stefan trusted his KLA colleague, he knew that the young man was more nervous than he would admit.

Nerves were to be expected in an operation like this, Stefan thought, as he quickly glanced back toward the lavatories. He got out of his seat, careful not to disturb the passengers around him, and moved towards the rear. The challenge was in conquering those fears— controlling them—so the mission could be executed successfully.

Stay calm, keep your head, and you'll do fine, Stefan had told his compatriots.

"Hello," he smiled at a heavyset flight attendant with mousy-brown hair. He hadn't seen much of this woman at all during the flight, and now she sat on a jump seat near the lavs. The woman looked tired, and it was all she could do to mount an effort to greet him in return. Good. The less alert these airline people were, the better.

He slipped inside a door marked 'unoccupied,' carryon bag in tow. *Stay calm.* Stefan repeated the silent mantra to himself. He was just a tourist, freshening up during a long overseas flight. Quickly, he bolted the door shut behind him. The lights flashed on brightly, and the din of the air vent kicked in over the whine of the jet engines.

Now, it came down to training and practice. He had to move fast.

He fumbled with his bag, retrieving among other items a large 35mm camera, rolls of film, hair dryer, and brush. He spread the materials out, using the floor, sink, and the lid of the closed toilet. But he kept the small counter clear.

From a shaving kit, he produced a small screwdriver and several pin punches. He'd executed this process countless times in rehearsal, as had Alex and the others. It didn't matter how many times he'd been successful. *Now* was when it mattered most.

Barely 90 seconds later, he was ready. The camera assembly yawed open like a gutted fish; the canisters of 'film' were open and discarded; the hair dryer and shaving kit lay in utter disarray. Stefan paused, leaning his trembling hands on the sides of the metal sink, and he gazed at his reflection in the mirror.

*Stay calm...*he thought, struggling to rein in his racing heart. Cool gray-blue eyes—only slightly bloodshot—stared back at him from an angular face whose damp paleness was accentuated by the jet-black hair and the harsh, fluorescent lighting.

It was a face he knew well.

The face of a patriot.

*Now then.* Stefan turned his attention to the narrow counter. There lay the components of a semi-automatic pistol.

Mishka and his technical engineering friends from the university had been right so far: the composite material of the barrel, slide assembly, firing mechanism, and frame had escaped the attention of the airport metal detectors.

Stefan had been insistent that the entire mission team should carry the broken-down components with them. At best, they would have four semi-automatic .32 caliber firearms at their disposal. At worst...well...maybe one or two of them might get through. But with the arrival onboard of his three colleagues, Stefan knew they'd all been successful.

The Kosovar reached for the makeshift pistol's grip; he was still amazed at the lightness of its ultra high-impact polymer construction. The magazine was of the same non-metallic polymer, designed to hold 6+1 cartridges, for a total of seven.

He delicately touched the cartridge jackets, lined up like soldiers against the mirror. They were made of a composite similar to the barrel and frame, filled with a powder designed for clean burn and maximum flash suppression.

When fully assembled, the pistol would be barely six inches in total length, small and light, with a minimum of recoil. It would also be deadly accurate.

Stefan looked in the mirror one last time. Elsewhere on the aircraft, now, or in the next few moments, the others would be going through the same assembly process. It was all part of the plan. With one exception. Stefan would have an extra 'goody' in his pocket. 'Insurance,' he called it, eyeing the disassembled travel alarm clock sitting on the counter next to the grip.

*Insurance.* He put his head down and set to work.

*\*\*\*\*\*\*\*\*\**

"I am soooo sorry!" Rebecca Hanson fluttered around Catherine Phillips, occasionally daubing at the pilot's dark blue slacks with a dampened cloth. The two women stood outside the forward lavatories—both of which were occupied at the moment—and Kate had her travel bag slung over her shoulder.

"Look...just *leave* it, will you?" and she held up a palm in warning. "You are giving me one hell of a headache, Hanson!"

Something in the taller woman's tone finally made the junior flight attendant stand down. She dropped her arms to her side, and Kate could not help but notice the dejected slump that suddenly appeared in the young girl's shoulders.

*What do you care, Phillips?* Kate asked herself, rubbing at her eyes with her thumb and forefinger. So she'd hurt the girl's feelings, so what? She wasn't the one who'd had pasta spilled on her, now was she?

With a quaking sigh, Becky ducked her head sideways, but not before the observant pilot saw pools of frustrated tears brimming in the girl's emerald eyes.

"Sorry," Becky said softly, and she began to move away.

*Oh damn...* "It's no big deal," Kate muttered. "I've got an extra pair of slacks—I'll just change, and it'll be fine."

"Are you sure, Captain?" Becky swung a hesitant, hopeful gaze to Kate, and it was then that the pilot realized the girl had thought she was in serious trouble. *Over some lousy marinara sauce?* In that moment of clarity, Kate understood that she had the power to either crush or encourage the flight attendant right then and there. Which would it be?

"I'm sure," Kate heard herself saying, "Really. It was an accident. Could have happened to anybody. Even Joan!" And she forced out what she hoped passed for a smile.

It must have, because she saw Becky's face light up in response.

"Thanks," came the grateful reply, and their eyes locked for a moment.

" *'Scusi!* "

Kate and Becky stepped back as the door to one of the lavs opened. Out burst a tall, firmly muscled Italian; he was well dressed and carried an expensive leather bag in one hand. He paused and let his eyes roam frankly up and down the long, curvy figure of the captain.

Kate returned his leer with an amused, speculative stare of her own.

"Another Campari and soda when you get a chance," he said, winking, before returning to his first class seat.

Becky was aghast. "Sir—" she started after him.

"Happens all the time," Kate cut in, reaching out and lightly grabbing the smaller woman's shoulder. Instantly, Becky's forward progress stopped.

"Some people don't even realize there *are* such things as women pilots. Just get him his drink, okay?"

"Okay." She shook her head and smiled, acceding to the captain's wish.

Kate found herself returning the smile, more easily this time. "Now let me get changed out of...dinner."

The two women chuckled and went their separate ways, neither one noticing the striking, blonde woman exiting from the second lavatory. She walked coolly, calmly, back to her first class seat, a small carry-on bag gripped tightly in both hands.

Outside the big 777-200, darkness had descended like an inky-black blanket, enfolding the aircraft in its deep, silent embrace. The winking navigational lights were overwhelmed by the depth...the completeness of it. Inside, night had fallen, too, with many passengers opting for sleep over the video.

So what was the harm? The Italian businessman chose to smile at the beauty as she passed by.

Alexandra Sadrio did not return it.

\* \* \* \* \* \* \* \* \* \*

Catherine Phillips did have a splitting headache, that was for certain, and she squinted her eyes against the lavatory lights as they flickered on. Quickly, she unzipped her leather flight bag, pulling out a fresh pair of regulation Orbis slacks, and she began to change.

She didn't get headaches often, she considered, slipping out of her soiled uniform. Stress was something she'd long since learned to deal with and put aside. It was a waste of her time. Not useful. Let others indulge themselves.

Kate had learned early about stress. There were the inevitable loud arguments late at night between her Irish mother and Greek father; money was tight, though the booze was never in short supply, fueling already strained tempers. It was all her father's fault, she'd heard her mother cry.

And then he had killed himself. Taken the easy way out.

Oh, Kate Phillips had found a way to deal with it, all right. No time to make any friends, she was too busy studying and training her ass off in high school so she'd be sure of securing that appointment to the Air Force Academy. It was jets that she wanted. To fly high and hard and fast. As if somehow she might find a way to outrun the demons that dwelled within her.

She never let up, not after she'd made the academy, not during that blasted physics class her senior year, and not during fighter pilot school afterwards at Luke Air Force Base near Phoenix. As quickly as she would achieve one goal and attain some small sense of satisfaction, she would start it all over again. Constantly increasing the level of the challenge. Testing the limits of the physical and mental demands she made upon herself.

What she hadn't counted on was her fair-haired little brother, Brendan, wanting to follow in her footsteps. And she had encouraged him to follow where she led: through school, into the Air Force, and into a career in the military.

Brendan had such a way about him, a joy for life and living, and at times Kate envied the way her brother could always be found at the center of any laughing crowd. He made friends easily. She did not. His temperament was mild and easy-going, while she was quiet and focused. Competitive as children, they were just as ambitious as adults.

Kate won her appointment to Colorado Springs, while Brendan had to settle for the ROTC program at Syracuse. Her little brother always ended up having to work harder and longer, pushing himself—taking risks—just to keep pace with his big sister. How they had delighted in teasing one another! Whether it was over who could run the fastest from the school bus stop to their row house in Queens, who could down more Coors at Martini's in San Antonio, or who would end up getting that plum opening in the test pilot program at Edwards Air Force Base.

More often than not, Kate would win.

Except for that last race.

He'd won the job and ended up losing his life. It was an accident, the Air Force panel said at the hearing. Accidents happen. Pilot error. Sorry. In memoriam, Captain Brendan Thomas Phillips. Great guy, we'll all miss him; here's his posthumous commendation, fuck you and goodbye.

Something in Kate had snapped then. A part of her felt as though she were to blame for what had happened. If only she hadn't encouraged him! She had let Brendan down, like their father had failed their family, and though she wasn't certain whether a life outside the cocoon of the military was for her, she sure as hell knew that she couldn't bear another moment within a system that she felt had failed her, too. Play the blame game, that was something the Air Force excelled in, she found.

Well, no more. And so she'd quit. Just like that.

She couldn't bear going home again, not after the angry way she'd left it those long years before, and so she was sitting on a beach on South Padre Island, Texas sipping a Coors, some three weeks later when the call came from Cyrus Vandegrift.

Somehow, her instructor from Luke had tracked her down. The old codger had friends at every level of the Air Force hierarchy, from the mail clerk at Luke to the four-stars sitting on their cans in the Pentagon. Equal parts taskmaster, friend, and mentor, Kate had allowed him into her life back at fighter pilot school. They'd stayed in touch for years, even after the veteran of three tours of duty in Vietnam had at last caved in and decided to go for the brass ring in the private sector as head of flight operations at Orbis Airlines.

"Just give it a shot, Katie," her friend had said. "After all, it's what you know!"

And so she had. Partly to please him, and partly because he was right: flying *was* all she knew. She was good at it, one of the best, and that was why Cyrus wanted her. She had loved it once, but Brendan's death had killed the part of her that held that joy. *Maybe the proverbial "change of scenery" would help me find the thrill once again*, she'd thought. And for a time, it did.

The hum of the 777-200's engines escalated in pitch, as the aircraft's flight director system made a slight adjustment in airspeed, chasing away Kate's ghosts. She finished dressing and turned on the tap, splashing chilled water onto her face.

Thirty-three thousand feet above the dark Atlantic was no place for a headache. She moistened a paper towel and placed it on the back of her neck. Maybe she would have Bill handle the principal flying duties for a little while longer, until she could shake this thing off.

The plane dipped slightly in the sky, and Kate had to reach out and grab hold on the side of the sink. The motion was not overly severe—probably in response to a bit of a down draft, the pilot guessed.

Over the muffled throb of the engines, she heard a second noise, closer: a clear, metallic clinking. She looked down, seeking its source. There, rolling in the bowl of the sink, was a small rod or pin, barely more than an inch or so long. Curious, she swiped it up before it could tumble into the drain, and she swiftly discarded her damp paper towel.

Turning her body slightly so she could examine the object better in the gray light of the lavatory, she twirled the pin between her fingers. It felt like metal, or something close to it. Machine tooled and crafted to specification, that was obvious to her trained eye. She swept her gaze around the interior of the restroom; nothing appeared amiss— equipment-wise or otherwise. Where could it have come from?

She looked again at the small pin in her hand, and an uneasy sense of familiarity crept into her belly. She flashed back to those days in training school and afterwards, when she was on deployment. Her Beretta 92 FS, or the 'M9' as the Air Force called it. She'd yawned through the lectures from her instructors and superior officers about how some-times a good pistol in hand was all that stood between a downed flyer and death or capture.

Catherine hadn't minded the fire-arms training she had received; in fact, she enjoyed the target-shooting aspects of it. But how she had hated the drills of keeping her weapon clean, of disassem-bling and reassembling it to exacting standards! Screw up on your own weapon, flunk the inspection, and you'd end up having to break down and clean your entire squad's. She'd ended up on the short end of *that* stick more than once, she smiled to herself. Even now, there were nights when she saw the com-ponents of the 9-millimeter pistol in her dreams. Some fun.

Maybe it's nothing, she considered, bringing the object to her nose for a light sniff, feeling slightly ridiculous as she did so. There had to be a thousand dif-ferent uses for such a thing, only one of which could spell trouble on her plane.

Kate sighed and slipped the pin into her pants pocket. She'd have to think about this for a bit. If only her head would stop pounding! She grabbed her flight bag, swung open the door, and headed back towards the cockpit.

She cast a quick glance towards the galley and the jump seat area. Rebecca Hanson was nowhere in sight. It was just as well. If the young flight attendant saw her, she'd probably want to make conversation or something. Small talk. As if they were friends.

*No way.*

Kate Phillips was quitting Orbis. The last thing she needed now was to make a friend.

\* \* \* \* \* \* \* \* \* \*

It was time. Stefan Bukoshi rose from his cramped coach seat, holding his small carryon ahead of him, so as not to jar it, and began to move to the front of the plane. All around him, passengers were in various stages of slumber: heads back or tilted to one side, mouths agape, huddled under the navy blue blankets of Orbis Airlines. It was well after midnight, according to these people's internal clocks, and Rome was still at least three hours away.

But Stefan Bukoshi, one-time politician-turned KLA member, soon-to-be hijacker, was on a different schedule.

He'd been keeping track. Four of the flight attendants were in the rear of the plane, chatting from time to time, or more often falling silent with the boredom. The other two had to be up ahead somewhere. Then there was the cockpit. He moved past the family who'd had the balky children's stroller when they'd come aboard—fortunately sleep had overtaken them all—up to his compatriot, Mishka Rhu. He took a chance, squeezing the man's shoulder as he walked by. Timing was everything, now.

Stefan slipped from coach into the business class section. He'd only had the briefest glimpse of it as he boarded the plane, but no matter. This was not his destination. Onward he moved, calmly, casually, through the murky interior of the plane, fully committed to a fundamental cause that the passengers who surrounded him probably knew very little about. And cared for even less, let alone be willing to sacrifice their lives for it, as Stefan and his team were. Well, they would all find out soon enough.

The tall, angular man silently pushed the first class curtain aside, and passed into the forward cabin. He was so close to the goal now he could taste it. It spurred him on, and he trembled with the excitement of it all. He slowed by Alexandra's seat, and she turned her head to him, sensing his presence. She was magnificent, with the blonde hair, the coal-black eyes, the passion for a cause that was exceeded only by his own.

Stefan turned his gaze several rows ahead, and there was Roberto, his first class seat fully extended in lounge mode, nursing a drink. *That buffoon better have his wits about him,* Bukoshi thought, and he intentionally nudged his carryon into the Italian's arm, startling him, as he passed by.

*There!* He arrived at the forward lavatories. Both were unoccupied, as he had hoped. Near the doors, the remaining two flight attendants, an attractive, older redhead and a young blonde, were standing, talking softly between themselves. They stopped speaking when they saw him and raised their eyes to him in a silent question.

The Kosovar was not caught unaware. He had expected to be challenged at some point, since he was not a first class passenger.

He offered the women a thin smile. "Emergency," he said, and he noticed the blonde's expression turn sympathetic. "And they're all full in the back." He kept going, pushing into the bathroom.

What would they do—stop him? Of course not. Easy-going Americans! But before the door closed shut behind him, Stefan took a furtive look at the door to the cockpit a few short meters away. Independence for his homeland lay just beyond it.

*********

"So, how many days do you have in Rome—two?"

"Three!" Becky said. She swirled a sip of cranberry juice in her mouth.

"Wow," Joan Wetherill replied. "Way, to go, Champ!" She turned and sat down on a jump seat, sighing. "You'll really be able to get some good sightseeing in." Off came her dark blue pumps, and she stretched her toes out. "But with Cindy and Nathan?" She looked up at Becky with a questioning, skeptical gaze. The older woman knew that Becky could get along with just about anyone. But being in close proximity to the Southern belle from Charleston and the boy from D.C. when they were on the cusp of being an "on-again" item...well, Joan could think of better places to be. Like her dentist's chair.

"You know, I've been thinking," Becky said, stepping aside as a tall, haughty blonde woman entered the second lavatory. The flight attendant had noticed her before in first class. Model thin, wearing tailored gray woolen slacks, a pale blue silk blouse, and charcoal blazer, Becky felt slightly intimidated by the woman, though she couldn't put her finger on why. The blonde ignored her as she slipped past.

Rebecca turned back to her crew chief. "I could stay at the Hilton..."

"With Cindy and Nathan..." Joan's eyes twinkled.

"Yeah," Becky laughed. "Or..."

"Or what?"

"Well..." the words came tumbling out, "There's this little *pensione* I heard about, on the Via du Macelli, near the Spanish Steps. I thought I might stay there awhile—you know, go native—and explore Rome on my own!"

Joan raised her eyebrows. "You? By yourself?"

"Sure!" Becky replied, slightly chagrined. "Why, I can take care of—"

"HELP!" They heard a woman's voice and a loud pounding on the inside of the lavatory door.

Joan leaped up from her seat, joining Becky outside the bathroom. "Are you okay?" The senior flight attendant rapped on the door.

"Help, me...please...I don't feel well..." and then a muffled groan.

"Open the door!" Becky tried pulling on the handle, without success.

"I caaaaan't..." Another ominous thump from behind the door.

Joan motioned her aside. "Here, let me try. And give Nathan and Alan a call, would you? Maybe they can help."

Wide-eyed, Becky nodded. In three steps she was at the call system, ringing the aft galley area.

"Ross," came the sluggish voice.

"Alan, we've got a situation up here in the forward lavatories." *Darn it, stay in control girl, will you?* Becky thought, noticing that her voice sounded an octave higher than usual, "and bring Nathan, would you?"

"I'm on it," he replied crisply, and severed the connection.

"Just slide back the bolt on the door above the latch..." Joan had pressed her head up against the door, talking to the unfortunate woman inside.

"I c–can't...I feel so bad...can't breathe..."

"Oh God," Joan said in a low voice, before adding, "Hang in there, help is coming!"

Becky noticed that several passengers in first class were stirring at the commotion, and Nathan and Alan rushing down the aisle towards the lavatories didn't help things any.

"What's going on?" Nathan's dark eyes flashed. He was all business now.

"We can't get this door open," Joan said tersely, "and the woman inside is very ill." She pulled once more on the latch.

"Huh?" Alan was baffled. "Ma'am..." He pounded on the door. "Have you tried the lock?"

"Alan!" Becky hissed, shoving him aside. "Of *course* she has. You and Nathan have to...to...I don't know–"

"Break it down," Nathan finished for her.

"Wait a minute." Joan held up her hands. Some passengers were standing now, and one—a large man, dark and well dressed—came forward.

"Can I help?"

"No sir; please," Becky said, recognizing the man as her Italian admirer, "go back to your seat." The man did step aside, but instead he moved out of the way towards the galley. And the cockpit.

The flight attendants continued to concentrate on the trapped passenger.

"We can't just break down the door," Joan insisted. "Can't you guys find something to pry it open with?"

"What? A fork?" Nathan started eyeing the door's hinges. "Get serious Joan! We'll have to bust it open."

Joan Wetherill's face was grim, and she shook her head. "Ma'am?" She knocked again on the door. "Ma'am? How are you doing?"

Nothing.

"Ma'am?" Worried glances passed among the flight crew.

"*Goddammit!*" Joan muttered under her breath. "Let me call the captain. We're gonna have to break this thing down."

\*\*\*\*\*\*\*\*\*\*

From his seat in economy, Mishka Rhu could see the two male flight attendants rush up the aisle towards the front of the plane. He knew where they were going. Four minutes had gone by since Stefan had squeezed his shoulder. They were right on schedule.

Mishka wore a hip-length black coat that he hadn't bothered to take off, choosing to leave it on to ward off the chill of the overseas flight. But the garment served a second purpose. He plunged his hand inside his left pocket and gripped the butt of his .32 caliber pistol. It had been simple, really, how easy it was for Mishka and his university friend, Ahmed Dushan, to design the components of a small but effective weapon that would escape security detection.

Ahmed was a good friend, so he asked no questions. Even if he had, Mishka would not have been able to answer him. For although Mishka was KLA and Ahmed was a KLA sympathizer, this was not a KLA sanctioned operation. Mishka didn't know who the money and the means were behind Stefan Bukoshi's plan, and he didn't care. He'd had enough of the war, of the atrocities. He wanted the Serbs *out* and independence for Kosovo. And the Americans had the firepower and the influence to make that dream a reality.

He held the gun nervously inside his pocket, and with a quick glance around the cabin, he started to move up. He hadn't gone far when the small brunette flight attendant pushed past him.

"Excuse me sir, would you mind returning to your seat, please?"

"Wha—"

But the woman flew up the aisle and did not look back.

Mishka Rhu swallowed hard, thought of his sister, of his parents, the faces of thousands of others, and he followed the flight attendant forward.

\*\*\*\*\*\*\*\*\*

"Sure you don't want me to check it out?"

"No, let me, Bill." Kate Phillips removed her headset and hung it on the side of her control column. "It'll give me a chance to grab a couple of aspirin."

"Still got that headache, eh?"

The pilot nodded.

"Okay. But let me know if you need any of my brute strength."

"You got it." Kate gave him a tired smile. "Back in a few."

\*\*\*\*\*\*\*\*\*

Stefan had heard one of the flight attendants call for the captain. This was a critical part of their plan. He couldn't have hoped for greater success! Carefully, he cracked open the door of his lavatory. From his vantage point, he could see the bathroom opposite him, the crowd of flight attendants and—to the right and back a bit—the door to the cockpit. Stefan opened the door wider and stepped out into the confusion.

"Ma'am, please, can you hear me?" More rapping and banging on the door.

Good. No one noticed his reappearance, as he had hoped. There was Roberto, standing further back, in the shadowed area of the galley. Stefan turned an eye to the cockpit door. If it didn't open soon, the mission would be more difficult, but not impossible. *We've planned for that, too,* he thought, fingering a small device in the pocket of his herringbone blazer. His carryon bag was over his shoulder now, and his other hand was behind his back. He swung his gray-blue eyes to Roberto, who dipped his dark, curly head in silent reply. They were ready.

The door to the cockpit swung open, and a tall, slim woman, her dark hair pulled back in a braid, exited. She wore navy blue slacks and a crisp, short-sleeved white blouse, complete with epaulets. Who was she? Stefan didn't care—the door was open, however briefly, and it was time for action.

The tall woman's eyes were upon the commotion at the far lavatory door. This was too perfect, Stefan gloated, and he began to move.

*   *   *   *   *   *   *   *   *

*Aspirin first, or that door?*  Kate half-considered the former, before shaking her head and taking a step forward. The door to the cockpit started to swing shut behind her.

In that last instant, Kate was aware of *someone* behind her, someone who shouldn't have been there. But she had no time to react, not before that awareness turned into a dark blur that viciously shoved her into the bulkhead, and bolted for the cockpit.

*What the hell?* Somehow, the pilot managed to keep her feet. But before she could even process what was happening, another shape loomed in front of her—a tall man, with narrow, hard features and a pale, barren gaze. The back of his hand connected with her face, hard, and Kate did go down then, with tears of pain springing to her eyes.

*This isn't happening. But it is,* she thought, feeling vaguely like a battered pinball.

She saw the dark loafers of the man move toward the cockpit, just as she became aware of the shouts and screams coming from the cabin.

"Everybody down on the floor—NOW—or I'll shoot!" A male's accented voice, Kate could tell that much through her cobwebs.

"But the captain—"

Is that Hanson talking?

"Move...move...NOW!"

More cries of terror from the passengers assaulted Kate's ears. *Not on my plane, dammit!* She struggled to rise to her feet.

The door to the locked lavatory opened at last, and a blonde woman stepped out, with an unsmiling, hardened look marring her attractive features.

"You heard him—*MOVE!*" Her voice was clipped, and she waved a pistol of her own.

"Who are you?" Joan Wetherill stepped forward, holding her arms back to keep Alan, Nathan, and Becky behind her.

"Move, or die." The blonde calmly pointed the weapon at Joan's head.

"Do it, Joan." Nathan put a hand on her shoulder. His voice was urgent. "These people are *not* messing around."

Joan gave the woman a withering glare, considered her options for a brief moment, and at last motioned her people to follow her.

Kate saw her chance now, while Goldilocks was distracted. If she could just get to the flight deck. The pilot lunged for the door, her head still spinning from the blow to her face. She tried to block out the gasps and screams of the passengers, tried not to listen to the struggle she now heard going on inside the cockpit, but it was too much. It was everywhere, all around her, the hellish roar of her worst nightmare come to life, blotting out the growl of the plane's engines.

Another shriek—*god, was that Hanson again?*—and then her skull exploded in a burst of shimmering stars. How pretty they looked, floating, drifting peacefully to the ground, and Catherine Phillips soon followed, into a field of shimmering light that quickly faded to black.

*Think I'll just rest here for a while,* Kate thought, not realizing she was helpless to do otherwise. And as the darkness closed in and surrounded her, she was able to register one last sound, coming from the cockpit. A short, popping noise that made her blood run cold. A sound she would've recognized anywhere.

Gunfire.

# Chapter
# 4

"Captain..."

A distant voice...so far away, yet so close, calling to her.

"Captain...please..."

There it was again! Like a drowning swimmer being towed to shore, Kate allowed herself to be pulled along by it, letting it lead her home.

"Ngghhh—" *Good grief. Is that god-awful sound coming from me?* There was no way to know, since she couldn't seem to detach her tongue from the roof of her mouth in order to form a question.

"Ssssh...take it easy."

There was relief in the voice now, Catherine could tell.

"You're gonna be okay..."

She tried to open her eyes, but they seemed to be stuck, too, and so the pilot decided to figure out whatever she could without the benefit of sight. She could feel the vibrations of the big 777-200 along the length of her body, so that meant they were still up in the air—thank God—although she must be lying down. Voices were arguing nearby in a language she didn't understand, and there were other sounds: lower, softer cries, or the occasional whimper. Something wet and cold, reminding her of a puppy's nose, kept pressing against her cheek and forehead.

"C'mon, wake up, please?"

There was that other voice again. So close. So familiar. So..."Ha-Hanson??"

Kate moved as she uttered the name...tried sitting up, and immediately she regretted it. Sure, her eyes snapped open at last, but little good they did her. Everything was a whirling blur.

"No-no-no!" Hands were pressing her back down, and Kate was aware now that it was a cool compress she felt, slipping off of her forehead—no, there...it was being arranged back into place again.

Kate blinked her eyes shut, squeezing them tight, and tried opening them again—without moving this time.

The strategy worked.

Now she could see the pale, concerned face and the green eyes of Rebecca Hanson hovering above her.

"How are you feeling?"

"What's going on?" The pilot ignored the young flight attendant's question, even as recent events came flooding back to her. Cautiously, she tried easing herself up on her elbows, and realized she was stretched out in a first class seat. The simple motion brought a wave of dizziness to her head and stomach, but she fought against it and remained relatively upright.

"I-I'm not really sure." Rebecca looked worriedly over her shoulder, and her voice was hushed. "They've moved all the passengers out of first class—this is a buffer zone here, I guess, and Cindy and Alan and the rest of us have been just trying to stay out of their way and do what they say."

"Joan?"

"She...she's taking care of Bill," Becky replied, and her voice broke at that.

"Wha—" Kate followed Becky's gaze to the aft section of the first class cabin. There was Bill Samuelson, her first officer, one arm hanging limply down the side of a fully extended seat, his head pitched back, his tie missing. The ghostly whiteness of his face stood in stark contrast to the vibrant crimson coloring the front of his formerly white Orbis shirt. Joan Wetherill sat by his side, rummaging through the galley's first aid kit, doing her best to staunch the bleeding. She whispered softly to him as she worked, but Bill's eyes remained shut. He did not hear her.

"Bill!" Fire surged through Kate's blood at the sight, and she sat up the rest of the way, releasing a loud groan in the process. "Dammit!" she muttered, bringing a hand to her head.

"Careful," Becky said, "you've got a nasty cut there." She lifted the compress back towards Kate's forehead.

"Enough of that." The pilot swatted the young woman's hand away. Someone had stolen her plane, shot her first officer, terrorized her passengers and crew, and given her one *hell* of a headache besides. Catherine Phillips had but one thought: to find out who and what she was dealing with. *NOW.*

Becky flinched back a bit. "Well," she said doubtfully, examining the angry wound, "looks like the bleeding's stopped at least."

"Who are these people?" Catherine swung her gaze around the first class cabin. There were Nathan and Alan, hands tied behind their backs, sitting sullenly on the floor near the galley. A sandy-haired man wearing a black jacket stood not far from them, pistol in hand. Cindy was next to Joan, helping her with Bill, while Trish Dugan sat in a seat nearby, crying softly.

Kate could see the fear that haunted their eyes—saw it in every one of them. It was no wonder.

"My name is Alexandra," a cold voice said.

Kate struggled to push the throbbing ache in her skull back to a more manageable level, as she turned to face the woman who emerged from the cockpit.

The tall blonde. Loud arguing was coming from behind her, and the pilot noted that the door to the flight deck had been propped open. The better to keep an eye on the prisoners, Kate guessed.

"Who is flying this plane?" The pilot demanded, struggling to stand. She felt Hanson's hand on her arm, attempting to restrain her.

"Stay where you are," Alexandra said, but Kate kept coming.

*"Stay..."* she repeated, as if to a dog, this time pointing her gun at the dark-haired woman for emphasis.

Kate stopped, and she could hear Hanson's sigh of relief.

Alexandra lowered her weapon. "I'm sorry I hurt you earlier. It couldn't be helped."

"Oh, really?" Kate shot the woman blue dagger-eyes, just so they understood one another. She could tell by what she found in the inky-black pools staring back at her, that they did. "Tell that to him," and she nodded towards her prone first officer.

A tall, thin-featured man wearing a herringbone jacket came out of the flight deck and carefully appraised Catherine with his gaze. "If your pilot had not resisted, we wouldn't have had to hurt him."

"He needs a doctor," Kate angrily replied. She turned to Bill, taking in his clammy features, his labored breathing. "Can we ask the passengers—"

"Already did, Captain." Joan lifted her head from her patient. "Can you believe it?" she laughed bitterly, "not a doctor on this plane."

"Let me have a look—" Kate started towards Bill.

"No!" the tall man waved her back with his pistol. "Leave it to her." He jerked his head towards Joan. "You all must stay where you are. He will receive help when we land!"

Kate tore her gaze away from Bill and exhaled sharply, her frustration reaching the boiling point. "And just who *is* flying this plane?" She was getting more worried by the minute. "Who...*what* are you?"

The man's slate-gray eyes narrowed. "My name is Stefan Bukoshi," he said, stepping closer to Kate. The pilot was a tall woman but Stefan bested her by several inches. Still, she did not back down. She held her ground against him.

"I am a patriot of the Kosovo Liberation Army, as are my colleagues." He waved his arms around the plane in a grand gesture. "We have issued a statement of our demands," Stefan continued, as if he were reading a press release. "You and the passengers will be released after we land, once those demands are met." He paused, turning his eyes towards the injured first officer. "Your pilot will receive proper medical attention, I assure you, after we arrive in Tirana."

"Where?" The confusion in Becky's voice was plain.

"Albania..." Kate breathed, answering for the Kosovar. She was beginning to get the picture.

"Do as we say," he said icily. "Listen to Alexandra and Mishka," he gestured towards the sandy-haired man, "and no one gets hurt." He spun on his heel and returned to the cockpit.

"Too late for that," Kate murmured, feeling the Hanson girl shiver at her side.

Kate understood her fear; hell, she was scared herself, though she would rather die before ever letting it show. At the same time she fought against a fury and an outrage that threatened to drive all common sense and focus from her mind. She needed to stay calm, to conserve her energy and to come up with some type of a plan. Because no matter what sort of a shipwreck she considered her own life to be right now, these good people around her didn't deserve to die.

And who the fuck is flying my plane?!

Catherine Phillips made up her mind that she would find out for herself. And soon.

\* \* \* \* \* \* \* \* \* \*

*"Merda,* Stefan! What were you thinking, shooting that pilot!"

Roberto Andizzi cast a furtive, side-long glare at the Kosovar before returning his attention to the maddening array of gauges and cockpit displays before him on the big 777-200. Sure, the fly-by-wire system made his job a relatively easy one. But it wouldn't have hurt to have a pilot with hands-on 777 experience nearby, in case he needed an assist.

"The pilot resisted," Stefan said, shoving his pistol into his belt. "You saw it!"

"I saw no such thing!" Roberto swore angrily. His directions had been to get into the pilot's seat as soon as possible, and he had done that, after giving the older man they'd found in the cockpit a good whack on the skull. He'd thought the worst was over with then, at least until Stefan stormed in behind him.

Yes, the pilot had struggled, but only half-heartedly. He, Roberto, had really knocked him for a loop. The next thing he knew, Stefan's gun had gone off. There was no reason for it. *It only made things messy*, he thought, glancing briefly at the spatters of blood on the cockpit floor. *What have I gotten myself into here?*

"*Merda!*" Roberto repeated, gripping the control column tightly. He considered himself a good pilot...had earned himself quite the reputation in the *Aeronautica Militare*. But the planes he was accustomed to flying—the smaller Fiats and Aermacchi MB 339s—were nothing compared to this jet. Once in a while he'd been able to get behind the stick of a big C-130 out of Rivolto Air Base, and it was for that reason, or so Alexandra had told him, that Stefan wanted him as a part of their team. But he had never considered the possibility that he'd be flying solo.

"What's done is done," Stefan said, moving behind the pilot's seat. "Now there is no turning back." He reached a hand to the control displays on a ceiling panel, examining them. For him, the discussion regarding the wounded pilot was closed. "Have we heard anything back from the authorities regarding our demands?"

"No." The muscles in Roberto's jaw clenched tightly. "Not a word."

\* \* \* \* \* \* \* \* \* \*

A glittering pair of blue eyes followed the hijackers' every move, and soon Catherine Phillips felt she had at least some sense of what their strategy was with the passengers. As far as she'd been able to determine, there were four hijackers. There were two in the cockpit, Stefan and 'whomever', although by process of elimination and based on what Hanson could recall seeing, Kate suspected that it was their Italian Lothario from first class. Additionally, there were two who prowled the first class cabin and beyond—Alexandra and Mishka. Since they were so few in number, the plan seemed to be to keep themselves out of reach of the 300 or so frightened and panicky passengers, concentrating instead on the nerve center of the aircraft.

From time to time, they would send one of the female attendants back into the main cabin, with instructions to do a quick sweep and calm the passengers.

During that time, one of the hijackers would stand at the top of the business class section, ominously brandishing a pistol, until the attendant returned.

Keeping Nathan Berbick and Alan Ross restrained by their own Orbis-blue neckties, sitting on the floor of the first class cabin on the starboard side, was again designed to control any potential source of resistance. Kate couldn't tell whether the two uncomfortable-looking men were more furious or frightened. *Probably a good bit of both*, she decided.

Just now, Alexandra had stepped back into the cockpit, and Mishka had escorted Cindy Walters at gunpoint out into the main cabin area for a passenger check. The Southerner had looked fearful, but she was holding up well in spite of it.

*All in all, the hijackers are shrewd enough*, Kate considered. Success—and survival—were at the front of the plane, and they knew it. *Maybe there's a way I can use that to my advantage*, the pilot thought, and then she turned her eyes to Bill Samuelson. Her heart skipped a beat. The first officer hadn't moved at all since he'd been shot. His breath was coming in shallow gasps, and his blanched features told of the amount of blood he'd lost.

"How's he doing?" Kate wanted to know, desperate to get him the help he needed.

Joan Wetherill stopped fiddling with a box of bandages and turned to Kate. The pilot could see that the senior flight attendant's nerves were frayed, her reddened eyes brimming with tears.

"Considering the top-notch medical care I'm giving him?" Her voice was bitter. "Not good." She turned back to the older man's deathly still form. "If I could just get this bleeding to stop..." A sob escaped her throat then.

"You're doing the best you can, Joan. I'm sure Bill knows that."

Catherine was surprised to hear Hanson speaking up beside her.

"He'll be okay, I'm sure of it," the young woman added.

"Thank *you*, Miss Pollyanna!" Trish Dugan snarled from her seat in the rear of the cabin. "Have you looked around here lately? A hijacker is flying this plane—taking us God knows where. Bill got shot and is probably gonna die. Terrorists are holding guns on us and they're probably gonna kill *us*, too—that is if they don't crash this plane first!"

Becky's eyes widened at this assault from such an unexpected source.

Trish continued her tirade, her face flushed and over heated, her voice reaching a near-hysterical pitch. "What I *don't* need is the likes of you pumping sunshine up my ass!"

"Trish!" Nathan shouted from his awkward position on the floor. "Shut up, will you?"

"Make me!" Trish screeched over the hum of the plane's engines.

A shocked silence descended within the first class cabin.

Finally, a low, rumbling voice filled the void. "What's your name?"

"You know damn right w—"

"WHAT...is your name?" Catherine repeated, cutting her off.

"Trish Dugan," the flight attendant replied, thrusting her chin out defiantly.

"Dugan..." The pilot blinked her eyes up to the ceiling and then down again, nodding. "I'm going to remember that. Listen, Dugan...." Kate pushed herself to her feet, ignoring the throbbing drumbeat in her skull. She leaned on the seatback behind her, facing Trish dead-on. "Knock it off."

"You can't—"

"Ssssh!" Kate cocked her head to one side, holding up a silencing finger. "Not a word!" she said, parting her lips to reveal a cold, chilling smile. "Got it?" She narrowed her eyes at the flight attendant. "Or *I* will personally shove something up your ass, and it won't be sunshine."

"Y-you wouldn't...." There was a glimmer of fear in Trish's eyes now, as she shrank back into her seat, trying to get out of the range of this wild animal that used to be her captain.

"Try me, lady."

Trish started to speak, but when the captain continued to smile, raising an eyebrow expectantly at her, almost daring her to utter a word, she backed down and clamped her mouth shut. With an exasperated snort, she swung herself around and stared silently at the inky blackness outside her window.

The tension broke. Kate released a sigh and lowered herself heavily back into her seat.

"Are you okay?" Becky touched a hand to her arm, and Kate could hear the concern in her voice.

"*Fine,*" she said too quickly.

"She's just scared, you know," Becky said softly. Green eyes looked up at Kate. "We all are."

"Scared or not, there's no reason for her to snap out that way," the pilot retorted. "It just makes things worse for everybody else." Not to mention, she thought, she didn't like the woman talking that way to Hanson. It just wasn't professional.

"She's wrong, isn't she?" Becky's voice was softer still. "We *are* going to make it, right? Bill...is going to make it?"

Dammit! Why was the kid putting her on the spot like this? "She's wrong," Kate said firmly, silently cursing herself for making such rash promises. "I'm going to get us out of this."

Kate could sense Hanson relax a bit, and she took some satisfaction in that.

"Good." Becky smiled at Kate's words. "I know he and Linda were planning a big vacation this summer for their 30th anniversary. He'd hate to miss that."

"Linda?"

"Bill's wife."

"Oh," Kate said. "I didn't know he was married. Uh...any kids?"

"Two grown sons—Jimmy got married last year—and a grandchild on the way." Hanson was looking at her curiously.

Kate coughed. "I...that's nice." How many times had she flown with Bill Samuelson, and never taken the time to find out anything more personal from him than the latest satellite weather reports? He was a first officer she respected and admired, and yet she'd never told him so. *Damn.*

"How about you?"

"What?" The pilot looked nervously around the plane, wondering if it were possible to change her seat while the hijackers were gone. This Hanson was making her entirely too uncomfortable.

"Do you have...any family?"

Kate hesitated a moment before answering. Did the young blonde next to her really want to hear all about her dysfunctional family? About her drunk, dead father? About how her own pride and ego had helped to get Brendan killed? At least she still had one brother left. Never mind the fact that they hadn't spoken in years. Or maybe the girl wanted to hear about the mother she still had in Queens. She lived only the East River away from Kate's Manhattan apartment, but they might as well have been an ocean apart.

Kate gave her the short answer. "No...not really."

"What's that supposed to mean?" Becky pressed.

*Dammit, why didn't the girl just back off?* Catherine released a sharp breath between her pursed lips. "It's a long story," she said. "I'm not married, if that's what you're asking." A pause. "How about you? Any family?" The pilot surprised herself, asking that question. All it did was serve to sustain this ridiculous conversation. What was the matter with her?

"Oh yeah!" Becky replied, brightening. "I was born in Los Angeles, and my parents still live there. I've got an older sister, Eileen, Johnny is my kid brother, and I've got two nieces—so far!"

Kate could hear the affection in the younger woman's voice as she talked about her family. "What are your nieces' names?" she asked through gritted teeth.

"Cally is five and Rebecca," she said proudly, "but we call her 'Becca for short, just so we keep ourselves straight, she was seven last month. They're

Eileen's kids. I love 'em so much! They are the *best*."

Becky hesitated, gulping hard, and then continued. "I promised the girls that I would bring them back souvenirs from Rome. I thought maybe...you know...a couple of those little miniature Coliseums...or else some T-shirts..."

Before Catherine knew what was happening, tears began to spill down Rebecca's face.

The pilot shifted uneasily in her seat. So Hanson was a weeper. Great.

"I-I'm sorry," Becky said, embarrassed. "It's just that I miss them right now." Quickly, she brushed the tears away with her fist, sniffling. "I'll be fine." She forced a smile. "Really...I will."

Catherine leaned back in her seat and sighed. *I'd better come up with a plan fast,* she thought, *before Hanson totally falls to pieces.* Still, there was something about the girl's pluckiness, her optimism in the face of danger, that the pilot inexplicably found herself drawn to.

"Both," Kate said.

"Pardon?"

"You'll get them both, Hanson. The miniatures *and* the T-shirts. I promise you that."

**\* \* \* \* \* \* \* \* \* \***

Stefan and Alexandra emerged from the cockpit together, a silent, conspiratorial look passing between them. A child was crying loudly in the business class section just beyond the closed curtain, and Alexandra moved down the aisle to check it out. Drawing her pistol, she swept the curtain aside and disappeared.

Stefan watched her go, frowning, and then he turned to face Catherine, his gimlet eyes running her through.

"What's going on?" the pilot boldly asked.

The hijacker sat down sideways on the arm of a seat across from her, and without a trace of emotion, he raised the gun to her chest.

"You came from the cockpit. You know how to fly this plane?"

"That's debatable," she replied.

In a flash she saw it, the back of Stefan's hand hurtling through the air towards her, but she had no time to react, no way to protect herself from it. The force of his slap whipped her head around sideways and partially shoved her into Hanson.

"Captain!" she heard the young woman gasp, and she felt smaller hands trying to steady her.

Kate slowly turned back to face Bukoshi. She tasted the blood on her lip. "Nice," she said, her tone low and threatening. "Look's like you've found something you're good at."

Stefan raised a hand to her again, and she could see the fury in his eyes, the purpling flush to his face, as he struggled to control his anger. Some semblance of sanity won out, and the man lowered his fist. "I ask you again," he said in a clipped, dangerous voice, "can you fly this plane?" And casually, as if on a whim, he turned the pistol towards Becky. He never took his eyes off of Kate, perhaps recognizing for the first time the danger she posed to his mission. "Well?"

"Yes," Kate replied, not hesitating this time.

"Interesting." It was apparent Stefan's mind was racing. "Now we understand one another. But to answer your question—Captain, is it?—we are still on course for Tirana."

"It'll be close," Kate said indifferently, and she had to raise her voice over the sound of the crying child in order to be heard. He was positively bawling now, and another infant joined in with gusto.

"What will be close?" Stefan stood, his irritation with the racket growing with each passing minute.

"Our fuel," Kate replied simply. Her ears were still ringing from Stefan's last backhand, but she knew well enough that if she could spark confusion and uncertainty among the hijackers, it couldn't hurt. "Tirana is a good 350 miles beyond Rome, over open water. I'm not sure what heading your boy in the cockpit has us on, but it doesn't take much for an inexperienced pilot to burn through fuel needlessly. I wonder at this point if we've even got enough left to get to Rome!" She turned away, dabbing at her lip with the soft cloth Hanson offered her.

"You..." Stefan worked his jaw, and his narrow face hardened. He was about to respond to the pilot, when Mishka burst back through the curtain. Alexandra and Cindy were nowhere in sight. The blood-curdling cries of the children were absolutely deafening now, and Mishka was clearly overwhelmed.

"Shut them UP!" Stefan whirled on Mishka. The younger man's eyes widened, and he shook his head helplessly.

"Alex and the stewardess are trying...C- Cindy thinks it's their ears..."

Stefan took a step towards business class, his eyes ablaze. "If you can't keep them quiet," he roared, then *I* will!" And with that, he shifted the pistol from one hand to the other, the butt of it facing out, and took off for the curtain.

*Damn, I must be getting slow,* Kate thought, for she had only just gripped the armrest of her seat when Rebecca Hanson flew past her. She raced towards the rear of the cabin, cutting off Stefan, throwing herself in his path.

"Hanson!" was all she could cry, forcing her aching muscles into a half-standing position. Kate could see Joan's shocked stare, and Trish Dugan let out an ungodly scream.

"No!" Becky raised her palms as if to ward off the Kosovar. "Please," she said, "leave them be. Me...Cindy... Trish...let us back there. There are over 300 frightened people who need our help! If you just give us a chance..."

"Return to your seat, NOW!" Stefan's voice shook with rage, and he flipped the pistol so that the muzzle of it faced Rebecca.

Kate had seen enough. She started to move.

"Stay where you are." She heard the unmistakable click of a pistol being cocked, and she looked across the cabin to see that Mishka had her in his sights. *Dammit!* The pilot froze, but her mind was on hyperdrive. *What is with this Hanson? Has she lost her mind?*

"Please," Becky was backing up as Stefan continued to press forward. "I'm begging you," and her voice cracked with emotion, "Leave them alone. They don't mean it. They're just children! Do whatever you want with me...they're the innocents here."

"Not anymore," Stefan hissed. He was scant inches from the young blonde, and slowly, deliberately, he raised his pistol to her face, using the tip of the barrel to trace a deadly line along her cheek and chin.

Catherine was livid. Who the hell did this creep think he was? And worse, she was furious with herself for not being able to do anything about it. Kate could see Becky stiffen, boring her green eyes into the hijacker. There was fear there, she could see, and anger, too. *I know a little something about that,* she thought, watching beads of perspiration suddenly form on Hanson's brow.

No one in the cabin moved. They were all ensnared in the standoff, mesmerized by the battle of wills.

"What are you going to do," Becky asked, her voice quiet and controlled, "shoot me?"

*Oh God...*Kate groaned. It was all she could do to not turn her eyes away from the disaster that was sure to follow.

Rebecca broke, but in a way Catherine never could have predicted: she kept her eyes level with Stefan's, and cautiously raised her hand to the pistol.

When Hanson's fingers lightly touched the gun, Kate was frantic. But Mishka's eyes were on the pilot, and his pistol kept her trapped in her place.

Instead, Kate could only stand and watch as a look of revulsion flashed over the girl's face, quickly bleeding into defiance. With a shaking hand, Rebecca carefully guided the muzzle sideways, until it was no longer pointed at her.

It was only then that the room began to breathe again.

"Oh, God," Kate heard Joan moan.

"Jesus Christ, Champ," Alan murmured.

"Stefan," Mishka kept his pistol pointed at Kate, "she's right. Let's use some of these women here to control the passengers. What harm could it do? This one-at-a-time, once-in-a-while...it isn't working!" His eyes darted from the pilot to the Kosovar.

Stefan Bukoshi's chest heaved in angry frustration, as he pondered that thought for a moment. He glared around the first class cabin, acutely aware of all the eyes upon him. Watching. Waiting.

"Very well," he said. "You..." he wagged his pistol at Trish, "...go with her."

"Thank you!" Becky breathed a sigh of relief, "You won't be sorry."

"Keep them quiet, Miss..." his eyes flickered to her name tag, "...Hanson," he warned, "or it is you who will be sorry."

It had been a long time since Kate had felt as helpless as she did right now. She watched Hanson nod at the hijacker, running a hand through her short blonde hair as she did so.

"C'mon, Trish," Becky said. The chastened, older flight attendant appeared to be in a state of shock.

"Let's see if we can't find those kids some juice," and she turned to leave. But before she did, with one hand on the curtain, she turned to look back at Kate and gave her a forced, 'see you later' smile.

The pilot felt the corner of her own mouth curl up, and she discreetly lifted her hand in a small, encouraging wave. She locked eyes with the smaller woman, holding her in her gaze, as if to will some of her own strength into the girl.

*God knows,* Catherine thought as Hanson disappeared through the curtain, *she's going to need it.*

\* \* \* \* \* \* \* \* \* \*

It wasn't until Rebecca Hanson began transferring ice from the freezer bucket into a tray of small cups that she realized she was shaking like a leaf.

She stopped what she was doing and steadied herself by leaning her hands flat on the countertop in the aft galley. *Calm down girl!* She concentrated on breathing deeply, on regaining her composure. The hum of the aircraft's engines, normally a soothing, centering sound to her, left her cold. Perhaps, because for the first time ever in her Orbis career, she wasn't sure just where she was heading.

*God, what is going on here?* In the last hour and a half, her world had been turned upside down. *Those people with their guns...they had come from nowhere.* One minute, she and Joan had been trying to extricate that woman from the lavatory; the next, all hell had broken loose.

There were the shouts and screams of the passengers, and Becky had to admit that her own had been among them, particularly after she'd heard that great crashing sound behind her. From the corner of her eye, she'd seen a blur of motion and of bodies, and then, to her horror, she saw Captain Phillips crumpled on the deck.

Becky had instinctively lunged for her, but that blonde woman had blocked her way. And Mishka...waving his pistol from the rear of the cabin...Becky had never been so terrified in all her life. So wild was the look in the young man's eyes that she feared the gun would go off at any moment.

She'd been too scared to move, and even more afraid *not* to, in those first chaotic moments when the hijackers had herded them together, shrieking for them to give in, to shut up, to get down.

And then there had been another burst of movement near the cockpit. It was the captain, shoving herself upright and staggering towards the door, in a last, desperate attempt to get back to the flight deck. When Becky had seen Alexandra react and deliver a crunching blow to the tall, dark woman's skull with her pistol, she'd felt sure she would faint herself. Until she heard the gunshot.

And everything changed.

In a flash of sickening clarity, Becky had realized that she would need to stay strong, to keep her head. She was responsible for her passengers' welfare, and she resolved she would do her damnedest to keep them safe from harm. Whatever it would take to insure their survival. Not to mention that of her fellow crewmembers.

And, if she got lucky, she just might make it herself in the bargain.

It was that determination that had galvanized her into action when Stefan had threatened those children. Becky hadn't stopped to think about the risks or the consequences. She had only known that she was all that stood between the hijacker and those innocents. She'd had to do something.

Becky felt slightly ill now, as her mind skipped back to that confrontation and what might have happened if Stefan hadn't backed down. She'd gotten lucky, that was all, and she shivered at that thought. It was unmistakably apparent to her that the Kosovar was not normally the 'backing down' type.

Becky reached for a pitcher of water and began filling the cups. The passengers had become calmer when they saw additional flight attendants moving up and down the aisles, almost as if they were providing normal in-flight service.

But the reality was that this was far from routine, Becky knew. She wasn't sure whether the captain had been telling the truth about their fuel situation—it had sounded plausible enough. One thing was certain, and that was that the pilot was quickly making an enemy of the lead hijacker, Stefan.

A knot formed in the young woman's stomach as she considered that fact.

The captain had sworn to her that everything would be okay, but right now Becky wondered just how she intended to make that happen. After the blows she had taken from the hijackers, it had seemed forever to Becky before the bleeding had stopped, an eternity before the captain's blue eyes had finally fluttered open after that first attack.

*Too damn much blood...*Rebecca thought, and she felt the tightness in her chest as she remembered how terrible Bill had looked when they dragged him out of the cockpit.

Becky picked up her tray of ice water and headed out into the coach cabin. She took a deep breath, steeling herself, forcing a smile to her face. She had to appear confident and calm to her passengers.

"Ice water?"

An elderly woman gratefully took a cup in a gnarled, trembling hand. "Are we going to die?"

"No...everything's going to be fine," Becky patted her shoulder reassuringly.

*The captain said we'd be okay.* Rebecca silently repeated the mantra to herself as she moved up the aisle. And in spite of how perilous things looked at the moment, there was something about Catherine Phillips' resolve, the determination in her voice when she spoke, the flash in her eyes, that made Becky want to believe in her with all her heart. As though it was perfectly normal  for her to have complete faith in this utter stranger. When she'd sat next to her in that first class cabin, she'd felt it. The confidence fairly rolled off of her in waves. Even when Stefan had challenged her, she had stood her ground.

*Maybe we'll get through this after all, just as the captain says,* Becky thought.

God, how she wanted to believe that.

# Chapter
# 5

Kate watched Mishka Rhu pace up
and down in the front of the first class
section, looking like a man who would
rather be anywhere else than where he
was. His eyes darted furiously around
the cabin, as though he were looking for
the nearest exit sign. He would check on
Alan and Nathan, then stomp back to
inspect the wounded Bill Samuelson and
the senior flight attendant who minis-
tered to him. The first officer still had
not stirred, but at least he appeared as
stable as possible, given the circumstances.

Periodically, the sandy-haired Mishka would squeeze his fists and dig down deep into the pockets of his black coat, and once he even produced what appeared to be a photograph from one of them. What concerned Kate most of all was the way the ethnic Albanian kept playing with his pistol, nervously cocking and uncocking it.

In Catherine Phillips' book, one should never pick up a gun unless one was fully capable of using it. She wasn't sure whether Mishka Rhu was. Not yet, anyway. Not from the clues she'd managed to pick up from him.

The young man was obviously in over his head, the pilot could tell that much. She'd seen very little interaction between him and Alexandra, and he seemed to be following Stefan's lead more out of fear and obedience, rather than anything else.

Kate sighed. She realized she was going to need help if she wanted to regain control of her plane, and looking to this frazzled Kosovar for assistance was as good a place as any to start.

"Can I have some water, please?" Kate was parched, and her voice certainly reflected that fact.

A pair of hazel eyes rested on her for a moment, and then Mishka silently turned towards the forward galley. A few loud bangs and bumps later he returned, cautiously handing Kate a cup of water.

"Thanks," she said, relishing the exquisite taste and feel of the cool liquid sliding down her throat.

Mishka began to turn away.

"Wait!"

He paused, regarding her questioningly.

"I-I wanted to thank you," Kate thought fast, "for convincing Stefan to let us help the passengers. I was worried," she lowered her eyes, "people could have been hurt."

"It was the right thing to do," Mishka gruffly replied. "Your little friend was right."

*Friend?* Kate thought the hijacker's choice of words odd, but she let it pass.

Suddenly, exhaustion seemed to flood through Mishka; he sighed and took a seat across the aisle from the pilot. Still, he kept his pistol drawn.

"I hate flying," he said glumly. He closed his eyes and swallowed hard.

The plane was vibrating more than it had in the last hour, and unfortunately

Kate had no idea why. She estimated that if the Italian pilot had maintained the airspeed programmed into the flight director, they were about an hour out of Rome. Tirana would be roughly on the same vector, on the far side of the Adriatic. It was still dark outside the windows of the big jet, but dawn would be coming soon.

"I can't say I would've given you a smoother ride." Kate offered him a weak smile.

Mishka grunted and looked away. Raised voices were once again coming from the cockpit, and it was obvious the Kosovar was trying to listen in.

During a lull in the argument, the pilot thought she'd give conversation another try. "Do you have any family in Kosovo, Mishka?"

Right question or wrong, Kate couldn't be sure, but it elicited an immediate, emotional response.

"What do you care?" he shouted, as pain and anguish seared across his face.

"I care," Kate said quietly, and she was surprised to find that she did.

Mishka ran the sleeve of his coat under his nose and turned a pair of bloodshot, tearful eyes to her. "I am here to win independence for my homeland. To avenge the slaughter of thousands of my people. But I can never bring back...Natasha."

"Who was Natasha?"

"My baby sister," he began to sob. "So young, so innocent...with her whole life ahead of her. And the Serbs killed her. Butchers!" he cried.

"I am so sorry." Kate reached her hand across the aisle and placed it comfortingly on his arm.

He did not pull away.

"But you have to help me, Mishka. Help me to understand what you're doing now. How does hurting these innocent people make all that go away?"

The Kosovar lifted his eyes to meet two sparkling blue orbs. He saw no guile in them, and for the first time during this interminable flight, he began to wonder if there might be a way out of this mess. *If only Stefan hadn't shot that pilot...*

Echoing Mishka's thoughts, the pilot nodded towards her first officer. "When does the hurting stop?"

She felt as though she had made some small strides with Mishka; the young man's face was a road-map of emotions, and in truth it pained Catherine to see the suffering and desperation that were apparent there.

"Stefan..." Mishka seemed to be at a loss for words. "Stefan says that by bringing America directly into the war, we will be able to force the Serbs out of Kosovo. We can't do it on our own! We don't want a 'NATO' peace. We will not rest until we have complete independence from Yugoslavia!" His voice rose with the passion of that last statement.

"Everyone wants to be free," Catherine said. "I understand that. But are you fighting for it in a way that would make Natasha proud of you?"

Mishka blinked, and turned away. "I never asked her."

"I don't think you needed to," Kate said. And a silence fell between them, as they each were left to their own thoughts.

After a time, loud voices again drifted in from the cockpit...words Kate could not understand. Mishka pushed himself to his feet, cocking his head and listened intently.

"What is it?"

The pilot was surprised when the Kosovar answered her, though he seemed to be speaking more to himself as he did so. "It's Roberto," he said. "He's tell-

ing Stefan that we can't go to Tirana
after all. The Albanians are refusing us
safe haven. We must fly on to Kosovo."

With a sharp hitch, Kate sucked in
her breath, turning to the blackness outside her window. For Captain Catherine
Phillips, this never-ending night had just
gotten a helluva lot darker. And even
more deadly.

\* \* \* \* \* \* \* \* \* \*

"You're mad, Stefan!" Roberto
shouted. "This is suicide!" The Italian's
dark features were flushed with anger.
"We can't just...fly into Pristina!
There's a war going on! And if I'm
reading this fuel display properly," he
banged the tip of a finger on the screen,
"I'm not certain we even have enough
fuel to make it!"

"Our Albanian brothers have turned
us away?" Stefan sneered, gazing out
the front windscreen into the blackness,
"We will show them! We *will* fly this
plane all the way to Kosovo. To our cap-
ital!" Stefan's eyes blazed. "That bitch
was lying to save her own skin. We must
have enough fuel! In a plane of this
size!"

"I'm telling you no, Stefan!" Roberto was panicking now. He never imagined that Albania would refuse them—weren't they allies, after all? And now, the alternative that Stefan was suggesting—to fly into the devil's mouth of a war zone—no way. Roberto Andizzi did not sign up for this. Surely his Alex would understand. He was refusing Stefan only to save all their lives.

They would be forced to leave this battle to free Kosovo for another day.

"To Pristina," Stefan insisted. "Tell them."

"Don't you understand, you idiot?" The veins bulged in the Italian's neck. "They won't even talk to me! They'll shoot us down like dogs, I tell you—and they'll be glad of it! We will be illegally entering Serb-controlled airspace!"

Stefan's eyes narrowed at the pilot's words.

"It's suicide..." he muttered again, desperately examining the display panels, wishing he could find a better solution in what the gauges and screens told him.

Just then, Alexandra returned to the cockpit. Other than the pistol she held, her cool, calm exterior gave no indication that she had been helping to hold an entire plane hostage over the past several hours. Rather, she looked as though she'd simply strayed out of a page from Vogue, in search of a canapé or two.

"What's happening?" She swung her eyes from Roberto to Stefan.

"Tirana is refusing us landing rights," Stefan explained, eyeing Alexandra carefully. "We are going on to Pristina. But Roberto here seems to have a problem with that. There is no reasoning with him, Alexandra," the Kosovar said in a hardened voice. "None at all."

A pause, and then Alexandra slowly, seductively, moved closer to Roberto.

"Roberto, darling, is this true?"

"We can't go to Pristina," Roberto cried out. "We'll be shot out of the sky before we can get ten kilometers inside the border! I won't do it, I tell you!"

Trying to figure out how to fly this blasted plane was one thing, but understanding his ravishing Alexandra Sadrio was another. She was a thing of stunning beauty. Closer and closer she came, smiling, and a wave of relief swept through Roberto. She understood him, clearly saw the logic of his reasoning, and he pushed himself back from the control column to welcome her into an unexpected embrace.

Yes, he thought, as he felt her lips caress his own, together they would stand up to Stefan. Later, after this was all over, he would find another way to help Alexandra free her homeland. But that would have to wait until after their holiday in Ischia.

"Alex...please..." he groaned, feeling her hands roaming along his arms, his back, tracing the line of his strong muscles. The sensation was electrifying. God, he and Alexandra were so good together! So what if Stefan was watching them? Let the bastard suffer!

The tall blonde's tongue danced with his, flicking, teasing, and then forcefully probing deeper, just as her hands moved around towards his middle, snagging his belt buckle.

"*Il mio dio!*" Roberto sighed. His woman's passion for him was insatiable!

Suddenly, Alexandra broke away.

Roberto was left breathless; his Alexandra had stolen away his wind with the heat of her kisses.

Alexandra smiled thinly at him; her lips still red from her assault on him.

"*Sciocco,*" she said, still smiling. *Fool.* She tapped the tip of his nose with her index finger.

"What?" At first he thought he had misunderstood. And then he saw her back away, still smiling all the while, only now she was holding a second pistol in her hand.

His. She had cleanly plucked it from him.

Dumbly, he regarded her, trying to process what he was seeing. *No...*

Alexandra was standing next to Stefan now. She tucked the additional pistol into the rear waistband of her slacks, hiding the weapon from view with her dark blazer. Then, in a move that rocked Roberto to his core, she leaned into Stefan, put her hand on the back of his neck and kissed him deeply.

After a few seconds that seemed more an eternity, Alexandra came up for air. She swiveled her head towards Roberto, an evil smirk now over-spreading her features. Beside her, Stefan too smiled. A cold, possessive grin that told Roberto he'd been bested. Alexandra was no longer his. If she ever had been.

"We are going home to Pristina," the blonde Kosovar told him. "Whether you are flying this plane or not."

That did it. *"Puttana!"* the Italian roared, lunging for her.

In a blur, the cold muzzle of Stefan's pistol jammed hard against his cheek, stopping Roberto in his tracks. The pilot was sweating now, staining through his expensive custom-made shirt. He squeezed his eyes tightly shut, fearing what was to come. How had he mistaken that trash for a real woman?

"You will fly this plane," Stefan said, his lips close against Roberto's ear, "or I will shoot you where you stand."

Roberto bobbed his head in agreement, feeling the pressure of the gun leave his cheek after one final jab. He opened his eyes and slowly made his way back to the pilot's seat, acutely aware of Alex and Stefan watching him.

So, he could die now, by Stefan's hand, or die later, at the business end of a Serbian surface-to-air missile.

'Later' sounded good to Roberto Andizzi. At least he would have the satisfaction of seeing that bastard and whore go down with him.

\* \* \* \* \* \* \* \* \*

"Mishka, what now?" Kate pressed. The commotion in the cockpit had risen in tempo after Alexandra had returned. "I can't understand it, but it doesn't sound good."

"Roberto doesn't want to go to Pristina...he says we'll be shot down."

"He's right," Kate said gravely, boring her blue eyes into Mishka. She was making a connection with him; she could feel it. But time was running out.

"Stefan...Stefan is...forcing him to do it." Mishka turned away and ran his hand through his hair. With a sigh, he began pacing again.

"Mishka, listen to me." Kate swung a quick, furtive glance at her colleagues around the cabin; they all were showing signs of the strain of being pushed to their emotional and physical limits. They couldn't take much more.

"You've got to do something," she continued. "We...have got to do something."

Hazel eyes met Catherine's in a glimmer of understanding.

"Don't you see?" The pilot rushed on, "We won't have to worry about getting shot down, we'll already have flamed out into the Adriatic for lack of fuel!"

The Kosovar hesitated. "I don't know...what if..."

"Look, Mishka, I'm a pilot, not a diplomat. But it seems to me that your cause is a just one. Your people have suffered terribly. But hasn't there been enough dying already?" Kate gestured towards the rear of the plane. "Threatening these people...leading them to their deaths...what kind of justice is that? It makes you no better than the evil you're fighting against!" She paused, gazing levelly at him. "Don't give in to it...like Stefan has."

"It wasn't supposed to happen this way..." Mishka's shoulders sagged, and he plopped down into the seat next to the pilot. For the first time, he lowered his pistol.

"Let me land this plane," Kate said firmly. "We can still save Bill...nobody else has to be hurt."

"I don't know..." Tears began rolling down Mishka's face.

"It's hard to live and work peacefully to see your homeland through to independence," Kate said, "but it's worth it, I think. Violence and death, that's the easy way out. It's your choice to make." *Wow,* Catherine wondered to herself, *when did you become such a philosopher?* Especially when she considered the fact that she had preached to

Mishka a doctrine that she herself hadn't always thought was true. When had all that changed? Catherine Phillips hadn't a clue.

With a soft sob, Mishka reached into his coat pocket and withdrew a battered photograph. A young, dark-haired girl, with an angelic, gap-toothed smile gazed up at him. "Natasha..." he cried. Cried, as he hadn't allowed himself to do since longer than he could remember.

\* \* \* \* \* \* \* \* \* \*

Alexandra Sadrio emerged through the cockpit door. The blonde, dark-eyed woman bore no signs of the drama that had just unfolded on the flight deck, other than running the sleeve of her blazer across her mouth. Mishka was standing at the front of the cabin, his pistol trained on Alan and Nathan.

"We're going to Pristina," the blonde said calmly, carefully eyeing Mishka for his response.

Mishka smiled thinly. "Home," he replied.

Alexandra nodded an affirmation. "Where are those stewardesses?" she complained. "They've been back there far too long!" She began to move past Mishka and Kate.

*It all hinged on Mishka now*, Kate worried. *Could he do it?*

The blonde passed Mishka and was walking just in front of where the tall pilot was seated.

And then it happened. There was Mishka, sweeping up behind Alexandra, chopping down on her pistol arm and clamping a hand over her mouth. The pistol fell harmlessly to the deck.

That was Kate's signal to spring into action. She lunged towards the woman, just as Alexandra shoved her elbow sharply into Mishka's gut.

"Oof!" He staggered backwards.

Kate rammed shoulder-first into the hijacker, driving her body back and over the top of a seat. The pilot followed her.

"Ohhh..." Kate heard a cry from the rear of the plane. Hanson, evidently, had reappeared.

"I see the gun," came Alan Ross's hoarse whisper. Mishka, as part of the plan, had freed him and Nathan of their bonds.

The wind was knocked out of both women, as they fell between the rows of seats. But the pilot had landed on top of Alexandra, and for a moment they both were still, locking eyes on one another, each appraising, ascertaining the strengths of the other. Kate, gasping for breath, was stunned at the level of hatred she saw in the blonde's eyes.

The black eyes narrowed. Suddenly, a bended knee came up, and the Kosovar planted a foot firmly in Kate's stomach. Back the pilot flew over the seats from whence she came, twisting, and landing hard in the aisle on her right side. *This one's not going down without a fight,* she thought, quickly scrambling to her feet, worrying that the skirmish would attract Stefan's attention.

And then she froze.

For the first time, Alexandra looked slightly the worse for wear. Her finely coifed hair was askew, and the shirttail of her silk blouse trailed down the side of her hip. Her chest heaved in fury, as she pointed a second pistol at Catherine.

Alexandra began swinging the weapon around the cabin, and she took a step towards the cockpit. "Don't move, anyone!" Her voice was a choking rasp.

Kate kept her eye on the gun. She rolled lightly on the balls of her feet, thinking fast, considering her options. Mishka was breathing heavily, just getting to his feet. Alan and Nathan had stopped dead in their tracks, the fear of ending up like Bill very real in both their eyes. And there was Joan, leaning her body over the unconscious pilot in a protective gesture.

"Don't, Captain." It was Hanson's voice, low and pleading behind her.

Kate swiveled back to Alexandra. She could see a flash of triumph pass over the woman's face...a gleam in her eyes. She was enjoying her victory.

*Dammit, this has to stop!* Kate thought, and she threw herself on the hijacker.

The gun was pointing directly at her. She could see Alexandra's finger whiten on the trigger.

Click!

Nothing happened.

Catherine barreled into Alexandra, taking her down hard this time, shoving her onto the deck. She had to admit it; she enjoyed the look of stunned shock on the tall blonde's face, wondering what the hell had just happened. And then she started to struggle beneath her. Kate hauled back and slammed her fist into the woman's jaw, and the resistance stopped.

"Sorry if that hurt you," Kate muttered grimly to the unconscious woman, echoing the hijacker's own words earlier, "but it couldn't be helped." She stood with a groan, dusting herself off.

"Whaa—"

Kate turned around to see an ashen, wide-eyed Rebecca Hanson.

"You are insane," Becky said, aghast.

"I've been called worse," Catherine grinned. "Actually..." she pulled a small narrow pin, about an inch long, from her pocket. She proudly displayed it to her slack-jawed crew. "...I knew the pistol wouldn't work without this."

"A firing pin." Mishka drew up behind her. He took the pin from her, examining it.

"Yeah," Kate said. "I found it in the lavatory after Roberto was in there."

"But how did you know whose gun..." Becky was having trouble following the pilot's reasoning.

"I knew Stefan's pistol worked," Kate soberly nodded towards Bill, "and you weren't in first class." She looked at Mishka.

"But still," Becky persisted, gazing at the pilot in wonder, "how did you know whether that was Roberto's or Alexandra's gun?"

Kate hesitated. "I didn't," she said simply, and shrugged. "But it seemed as good a time as any to take a chance."

Becky closed her eyes and breathed deeply. *Stay calm...stay calm...*she chanted to herself, holding onto a nearby seat back for balance. This Catherine Philips was just crazy enough to maybe save all their lives.

"Tie her up and keep an eye on her," Kate said to Mishka. She moved closer to the Kosovar. "You okay?"

He gulped hard and nodded an affirmative.

Catherine gave his arm a gentle squeeze. "Ya done good. Now," steel-blue eyes flickered towards the cockpit, "I'm gonna go get my goddamned plane back."

\*\*\*\*\*\*\*\*\*

There was no time to waste. Kate cautiously approached the flight deck, silently motioning to Alan and Nathan behind her. They had their instructions. She would go for Stefan. They would follow after she'd disarmed him— she wasn't quite sure how yet—and get him out of the cockpit. They'd have to make sure Roberto wasn't giving them any trouble, either. But after what Mishka had heard earlier, she doubted it.

*Mishka...*Kate's heart went out to the young man. He'd simply been caught in the wrong place at the wrong time. Given similar circumstances, Kate wondered whether she might've done the same as he. She would never know.

She had asked Mishka and the rest of her crew to steer clear of the cockpit unless absolutely necessary; with so much delicate equipment in the 'front office' needed to fly the big bird, the last thing she wanted was to see any of it damaged.

The pilot breathed in through her nose and out through her mouth several times in quick succession, energizing herself. She nodded reassuringly at Alan and Nathan. The young men looked scared, but also determined to help wrest control of the plane back from the hijackers. This was the only chance they would get.

Catherine felt cold. Goose bumps peppered her forearms, a result of the chilled air being pumped through the cabin by the plane's environmental controls. She had to remember to adjust them once she regained her pilot's seat. Her hands were cold, particularly the one that gripped the butt of the pistol to which she'd just added the missing firing pin. And there was a calm, calculating coldness in her mind...the pit of her stomach...the beating of her heart. She'd found it best in the past to enter such a state of focused, heightened awareness prior to undertaking any mission. In her mind, by separating herself from her emotions and from those of the people around her, she was more effectively able to achieve her objective. Never had she needed that skill more than at this very moment.

The tall, dark woman silently mouthed, "NOW!" to the men, and she ducked into the cockpit, pistol drawn.

There was Roberto, sitting at the controls. The Italian spun around in his seat, nervous perspiration dotting his brow, and a stricken, sickly look on his handsome features.

Where the hell is Stefan?

Too late, Catherine realized something must've tipped him off. She followed Roberto's wide, green eyes to the cockpit door.

*Shit!* Stefan had been behind it. The door swung forward, hard, smashing into Kate's side, throwing her into the bulkhead. The pilot watched helplessly as her pistol was jarred loose and flew to the opposite side of the cabin.

She recovered quickly, knowing her life depended on it. She moved towards Stefan, catching the maddened gleam of fury in his ghostly eyes, and she watched him take aim with his pistol.

Kate felt herself slightly lose contact with the floor of the plane, as it dipped in the sky. That damned heavy air again, but she welcomed it this time, because it was just enough to temporarily throw Stefan off-balance. He flailed his arms wildly, and Kate heard the sickening *pop!* of a shot plunk into the insulated ceiling of the plane. Taking advantage, she swung her foot into the air, landing it solidly on his wrist. Now it was the hijacker's turn to be disarmed. *Thank God for 'Unarmed Combat'!* wisped through her brain. That course at the Academy had been a guilty pleasure of hers.

"You!" Stefan roared in pain, backing away, fumbling for something in his coat pocket.

"It's over, Stefan," Kate growled, moving in close. Was he carrying another weapon? She couldn't be sure. At the same time, she desperately tried to track down the other two guns in the cockpit. "Don't even think about it, Roberto," she called back over her shoulder.

"No...no-no-no..." came the anguished cry of relief from behind her. "*Grazie Dio*...thank God you are here!"

Stefan stumbled against the starboard bulkhead, as turbulence once again rocked the plane. "I said stay back!"

"No way," Kate countered, holding up a warning hand towards the cockpit door. It was too soon for the young flight attendants, not until she'd broken Stefan. "Mishka's given up!" And then, thinking *Why not?* she added, "Alexandra has, too!"

"You're lying," he growled, spittle flying from his mouth.

"Why don't you go in there and ask them?"

"NO!!!" And then Stefan found what he was looking for. He whipped from his pocket a small device; to Kate it reminded her more of a travel alarm clock than anything else. However, judging by the curled red and blue wires dangling from the back of it, she feared it was anything but.

"I will blow this plane from the sky!" He shook the device at her, his thumb poised over an orange button. "I swear it!"

*Fuck!* The pilot thought. Could it be a bomb—really? How could one have gotten aboard? With all the security checks at JFK and at Orbis...impossible. Still, the hijackers had somehow managed to get those modified firearms on the plane. Was it too big a stretch to consider they'd done the same with an explosive device? Kate shuddered at that thought.

"Stefan—no!" Roberto shrieked.

"Keep your hands on that stick, Roberto!" Kate warned.

"*Si...si bella!*"

She returned her attention to Stefan. "Give that to me," she said, as she stepped in closer.

"Keep back!" he screeched, shrinking into the bulkhead.

"Look around you." Kate waved her arm, her heart pounding in her chest like a trip-hammer. "It's all over."

Stefan shifted his eyes from the cockpit door, to the front windscreen, and finally back to the tall pilot. First, his homeland had rejected him, then his allies, and now his friends and his lover. He, a man who once thought he had nothing to lose, had lost everything.

Almost.

Stefan's lower lip trembled slightly. Taking in a great gulp of air, he made his decision. If this was a battle he could not win, then neither would anyone else.

"It's over," Kate repeated, reaching out her hand to receive the detonator.

"Not yet," the Kosovar replied, and his thumb pressed down on the button.

The hackles on the back of Kate's neck stood up, and she froze, listening. For a moment, she thought the hijacker had been bluffing after all. They were all right! And then she felt a dull thump, coming from deep within the bowels of the plane. The muffled sound of it reminded Catherine of the times when she'd accidentally run her jeep over those dumb jackrabbits on the night highway outside of Luke.

In the split second that followed the thump—nothing happened. Kate turned a pair of startled, blue eyes to Stefan. She could see the confusion on his face. Obviously, this was not the outcome he'd been hoping for.

The pilot reached out for the Kosovar. "You're coming with—"

She never finished the sentence.

Kate felt her body lift from the deck of the cockpit, and she found herself suspended in a weightless ballet before she was roughly thrown down to the floor. The back of her head crunched against the thinly carpeted floor.

"Aaah!" she cried out, seeing stars. She lost track of Stefan.

Screams. Roberto's? Her own? And then the harsh, grinding, metallic sound of something giving way. Like two wrecked bumpers scraping apart...or a fuselage being rent open.

Kate was rolling now, spinning towards the rear of the cockpit. In spite of the labored whine of the engines, the warning klaxons, the confusion of her spatial disorientation—her pilot's training told her very well what was going on.

The plane was in a dive.

\* \* \* \* \* \* \* \* \*

When she heard the shot fired, for the second time during the dark night Rebecca Hanson felt terror and helplessness wrench at her gut.

Trish Dugan yelped as though she had been the one fired upon.

"Oh no..." Cindy Walters' face paled, and she gripped Joan's arm, hard.

Mishka could not help it. With one look at Alexandra still slumbering peacefully, he started to move towards the cockpit.

Later, looking back on it, Becky wasn't able to recall what inner force made her propel herself towards the front of the plane, what compelled her to push past Mishka, fighting the turbulence, stopping short only when she came up on Alan and Nathan crouched outside the cockpit door. She only knew that Captain Catherine Phillips was busy trying to save all their lives while risking her own, and she simply couldn't stand by and do nothing if the taller woman was in trouble.

"Christ!" Alan swore. He spun around, grabbing Becky by the arm. "What the hell are you doing up here? Get back!"

"What's happening?" Becky tried to control the anxiety in her voice. "I heard a shot."

"That bastard Stefan!" Nathan's dark eyes sparkled with both excitement and fear. "He tried taking a shot at the captain. And now..."

"We think he's got a bomb!" Alan finished for him; his tanned face had turned unusually sallow.

"No...we've got to help her!" Becky tried to wrench from Alan's grasp.

Loud voices and a crash came from within the cockpit, then conversation, tense, and in lowered tones.

"Not yet!" Nathan hissed. "The captain hasn't given the signal!"

"Let me go!" The little blonde again tried pulling away, until she felt a rumble and a thud coming from beneath her feet. She froze. Not a good sign, feeling the floor undulate beneath her feet.

"What the *fuck* was that?" Nathan swiveled his head around the cabin, looking for the source of the sound.

Becky took advantage of her colleagues' confusion, and she tugged herself free.

"Something's wrong." Her voice was hard, and her green eyes blazed at the men, challenging them.

Alan sighed. He knew he'd been beaten by the young Californian. She sure had one hell of a backbone for such a little thing! "Let's go," he motioned to Nathan, "and you wait here, Champ, okay?"

Alan stood still, his warm blue eyes looking down upon her, waiting for her answer. In retrospect, Rebecca was sure she would have said 'yes.' It was just that she wasn't given a chance to do so.

For there was no time for words, only the beginnings of a breathless scream, when the floor fell away from beneath her feet.

\* \* \* \* \* \* \* \* \* \*

*Oh God...*G-forces kicked in, pinning Catherine to the rear bulkhead like a wrestler to the mat. All sorts of debris flew by, blinding her: dust, papers, a gum wrapper. The breath was wrenched from her lungs, choking off any words...robbing her of her strength. The pilot didn't know how severe the hull breach was, but the one thing she did know was that the only way they would have any chance at all was if she could make it to the 777-200's control column.

Slowly, agonizingly, she began to inch her way across the flight deck, plotting a course for the pilot's seat. She could see that Roberto had been thrown to starboard side of the cockpit, close to the first officer's position.

*Good*, she thought grimly. *I don't have to actually kick him out of my seat!* The pilot clawed at the woolen carpeting, straining...pulling on the soldered-down instrumentation panels, the frame that held the leather seats. She wasn't sure if she could actually smell smoke or if she imagined it, but just the hint of it creeping into her awareness jolted her with that last burst of energy she needed.

With a defiant cry issuing from her throat, the pilot heaved herself into her seat, shoving the dangling oxygen mask aside. Many of the matrix displays either vibrated with incomprehensible data streams and warning flashes, or were entirely blacked out. Kate instantly understood that whatever other damage the blast had done, it had blown out the main electrical buses on the fly-by-wire system. All programmed controls and safeties were off. What flying remained to be done would be hands-on, from here on out.

Thank God the artificial horizon was still working, but Kate's senses were already telling her what she needed to know. The diving plane was steeply banking to the left. Desperately, she jammed her foot on the right rudder pedal, so hard she thought she might punch a hole through the floor. She trimmed the right ailerons all the way, and she heard in response the wind screaming out a protest against the over-stressed wings. Finally, with a whisper of a prayer to a god she wasn't sure she believed in, she pulled the control column up as far as it would go, desperately hoping that the nose of the diving 777-200 would respond.

It was a last ditch maneuver, she knew. Trying to trade airspeed for altitude this way, forcing the fuselage to its very limits, was a fool's gamble even if her plane had been whole. In the nightmare of her mind's eye, Kate visualized the great wings of the Boeing jet ripping away from the airframe, surrendering to the immutable laws of physics. Then it would be a race between the wings and the main fuselage to see which would slam into the rock-hard ocean first.

"C'mon..." Kate willed the nose up. The aircraft heaved and shook, indignant at being flown in so outrageous a fashion, and the roar of the big PW4098 engines began to drown out the tornado winds in the cockpit.

"Do it..." The pilot's hands rattled violently on the control column; the balky stick was rudely trying to throw her free. But Kate had already decided that one way or another, her hands were not leaving the controls of this plane. Her passengers' lives were at stake.

People who didn't deserve to die. People who had earned a second chance...the image of Mishka flashed before her eyes...and people whose lives had barely begun. People who had so much more living left to do...Hanson, for instance.

There! What was that? Kate thought she'd detected some slight change in the aircraft's attitude. A quick check of the artificial horizon confirmed it. They had started to pull out of it!

"Go baby, go!" Kate could feel it now, the roiling of the blood in her veins that told her she had become one with the beast, had merged with it for a time, so as to save them both.

The pilot could see the gossamer-tipped whitecaps of the ocean below, glimmering in a pre-dawn glow, but the waters were not racing up quite so fast now.

"Unnhh..." Roberto started to regain his senses. He held the back of his head while scrambling into the co-pilot's seat. "Wha—"

"Later," Kate shouted over the engines, her hands still in a white-knuckled death grip upon the sluggish wheel. It was like driving a fully loaded semi-trailer without power steering,

Kate thought. The ferocity of the dive was terrifying. She swore she could hear the airframe's rivets popping free, smell the brine of the salt waters languidly pulsating below.

After hours-long seconds, she felt the pressure on her aching back muscles ease, as the G-factor reduced in response to the plane's leveling off. Finally, she had it! The plane pulled out of the dive, and not a moment too soon.

Kate released the breath she hadn't realized she'd been holding. They were alive, for the moment anyway. Now, she had time to fully grasp the extent of the countless problems shouting at her from the control panels. But which indicators should she trust?

A visual check out her starboard windscreen told her one flashing warning was very real: a fire in the number two engine. The blast must have splintered an oil or fuel line tracking through the wing. Without the aircraft's fly-by-wire, it was difficult to tell. But the regulation response was a no-brainer. She flipped the cut-off switch to the engine, watching with relief as the fire sputtered and flamed out.

Their odds for survival had just gotten worse.

Under normal conditions, the plane could remain airborne with only one engine. But now...without knowing the fuselage damage, let alone how the explosion had affected the plane's hydraulics, the pilot was worried about an engine stall or a rudder hard-over. Each was a distinct possibility with reduced airspeed and manual flying.

"Saddle up, Roberto," Kate gestured to the flight controls. "I'm going to need all the help I can get."

Motion. The rear of the cockpit. It was Stefan again. Didn't that guy know when to stay down? Crawling along the floor...of course! He was reaching for a pistol wedged against a rear jumpseat.

Not good. There was no way she could leave her seat now, and still keep this plane in the air. She was helpless.

*Dammit!* she cursed to herself, as the plane started shuddering. *What now?* She could barely read the instruments vibrating on the panels.

"Yeeeaah!" In through the cockpit door, burst Alan and Nathan. Bless their Orbis hearts, she was never so happy to see a flight crew in all her life.

"Get Stefan out of here!" Catherine growled, but her request was unnecessary. Out of the corner of her eye, she could see Alan and Nathan tackle the hijacker, one leg each, as if they were playing in a rugby scrum.

Stefan almost had his fingers on the tip of a pistol, when the force of the men on him, together with another hit of air turbulence, pulled his hand up short. The weapon slid away from his outstretched grasp.

"Watch the gun!" Nathan's voice.

Kate fought to control the plane as it began to push into a right-hand turn, driven by the single port engine.

"I see it!" Alan sang out, but the Kosovar saw it, too. The plane chose that moment to roll sharply right, then readjust itself as if it had a mind of its own. With a violent kick, Stefan managed to free one leg and shove Alan back on his haunches.

The jarring rattle of the aircraft sounded as if it were hitched to a runaway train, fighting Kate every inch of the way, as she frantically toggled and tested the controls she could get to.

"What do you want me to do?" Roberto's shirt was drenched in sweat now.

Kate spared him a quick, no-nonsense glare. "*Exactly* what I say. Nothing more, nothing less."

The Italian pilot gulped and nodded, staring down at the displays.

Kate worked the rudder pedals furiously. "C'mon...."

The plane rolled again, not as severe a motion as the last, but it was enough for the pistol to slide across the decking and directly into Stefan's hand.

"He's got a gun!" Nathan's voice rose an octave.

"Watch out!"

"Shit!"

"What the—*Becky!*"

Catherine's head swung around sharply at that and then, to her eye, everything began to roll in slow motion.

Rebecca Hanson, rushing through the cockpit door. Her green eyes sweeping around the flight deck, taking it all in, making contact with the pilot's own sea-blue gaze, then moving on to the pistol in the hijacker's hand.

Stefan twisted on the floor of the plane, bringing Kate into his sights.

A wild-eyed look on Nathan's face...the young man lunging for the weapon.

But Catherine Phillips already knew he would be too late. The airplane's stick began to shudder in her fist. More warnings blared uselessly into the cockpit. A stall was close at hand.

*Nooo!* Kate had never felt more helpless in her life, yet still she continued to fight it. "C'mon you bastard!" she shouted at the control column, and she was forced to push the nose down again, generating airspeed. At the same time, she braced herself for the ripping impact of the bullet she knew was coming.

The crackle of gunfire, more shouts—and Kate was surprised to feel nothing after all. But she heard it...a soft cry behind her, and a thud.

"Becky!" Alan's croaking voice.

Anger, fear, and concern exploded in the pilot all at once. A desperate, quick glance behind her told her more than she needed to know. There was Hanson, slumped on the floor; a red, sticky wetness over-spreading the white, left shoulder of her blouse.

"No..." Kate groaned aloud, closing her eyes briefly against a vision that was wrong...all wrong. It should have been her laying there, not the young blonde. *Damn you, Hanson!* She fought back the growing, fluttering panic in her stomach, tried to overrule her lurching heart with all the practical sense she could muster. *I'm not worth it!*

Too late Nathan reached the gun and unleashed a blistering uppercut to Stefan's narrow, angled jaw. "Fuck you...fuck you..." the young flight attendant sobbed, pounding on the terrorist.

The stick was shaking so hard in Kate's hands now, she feared that her teeth might rattle out of her head. She did a quick inventory: hijackers out of commission—good; explosion onboard, major digital systems out, manual systems sluggish—not so good; first officer wounded, one engine dead, and Hanson...she pushed that thought out of her head.

By God, she still had one engine that worked. A rage boiled up within her, and a passion, a hunger for survival did, too. Whether she could attribute it to her Celtic mother, her Greek father, or a hybrid of both, she did not know. But as long as the plane had power, she had a chance.

After all they had been through, after all that had been ventured and sacrificed, she had no intention of losing this plane now.

"Alan...Nathan..." she shouted over the din, "get them out of here..." and looking at Hanson's pale face, "and help her..." She fought the tremor in her voice at that. Wordlessly, Alan was already scooping the young woman into his arms.

Kate swallowed hard and turned back to her controls. She stared out over the open water, her blue eyes mirrored in the ocean glimmering below.

"Prepare for an emergency landing. And *shut* my goddamned door!" There was a *bang!* as the door thwacked closed, and they were gone.

"W–wh–where are we landing, *Capitano*??" Roberto was in a near panic.

The pilot checked her few working displays, absorbing what the readings told her. *Screw it all, I'm bringing this bird in on time!* Her eyes narrowed.

"Rome."

# Chapter 6

Captain Catherine Phillips idly regretted that the Boeing's comm system was still working. She forced herself to pay little mind to the frenetic chatter of the Fiumicino Tower controllers in her headset. What could they really do to help her now, anyway?

She'd told them to clear the airspace between her mark and the airport, to give her their longest runway, and to have emergency vehicles on-hand. Catherine hadn't wasted time on the details, she'd simply told them the basic facts of their status: the hijackers were no longer in control, there had been an explosion—

extent of damage unknown—and be pre-
pared to receive injured people.

The big plane would be coming in
heavy and hard, and the pilot had no idea
if the hydraulics that remained would
enable her to maintain any sort of control over the flaps and rudder, let alone
the wheels and brakes. And all on manual...she would need every bit of Roberto's help when they got to Fiumicino.

*IF* they got there. Catherine estimated they were still about 10 minutes
out.

The aircraft had just skimmed over
the rocky hills of Corsica. The island
had risen out of the ocean like a sepia
and bronze-colored elbow patch, jag-
gedly stitched into the deep blue waters
surrounding it. Kate squinted into the
eastern sky, raking her eyes over the
horizon, knowing that her destination
was out there somewhere.

She'd been able to maintain a fairly
level flight at 8,000 feet over the past
few minutes. Less room for error should
something else go wrong, but for the
comfort of her passengers, it was a risk
she had to take.

The cockpit was bathed in the faint
light of the distant sunrise and the doz-
ens of warning lights glowing from the

controls. One such warning had indi-
cated a fire in the starboard cargo container, and she'd had Roberto activate
the fire suppression measures in that
compartment. Kate guessed the hold
probably had been where the bomb went
off.

*Grazie Dio...*Roberto sighed. The
fire suppression system must still have
been on-line, because the warning light
winked out.

The Italian's swollen eyes ran across
the display panels, hopelessly, before he
turned them to Kate.

"So much of this...it's not working!"

"We've got enough," Catherine
mumbled to herself, as the aircraft once
more began to buck and roll beneath her.

"Dammit!" The sole port engine was
again pushing the plane into a hard
right-hand turn, and Kate feverishly
tried to manually compensate. "The rudder!"

"Si!" Roberto's voice was raw. He
instinctively turned his control column
to the left, extending the ailerons and
spoilers on top of the wing. Unfortunately, it was the wrong maneuver for
the damaged plane.

Instantly, the aircraft's drag
increased, and the nose bobbed up.

"What the..."  Kate's voice could barely be heard over the dreaded 'stick shaker' warning.  The Boeing was going so slow now that a stall was a distinct possibility.  "Just use the rudder on the goddamned tail!" she angrily swore. Using the tail rudder alone, Kate knew, the jet normally should have banked back to the left.  But with the additional slowing element of the spoilers, airspeed was dramatically reduced, and so their direction of travel remained unchanged.

"Push down!"  Kate shouted, jamming the control column forward, pitching into a dive, in a desperate attempt to increase their airspeed.  At the same time, she furiously worked the rudder pedal, determined that the plane would accede to her directional demands.

The 777-200 dove through the sky, falling towards the blue-green waters where the Ligurian Sea met the Tyrrhenian.  Faster and faster the waters rose up to welcome them, glowing and gleaming under the low, rising sun.

6,000 feet.

5,000 feet...3,000...2,000...and at last the stick stopped shaking.  But now they were too damn low.  "Pulling out of it!"  The dark-haired woman yanked back on the control column.  Still, they were skidding to the right. *What the hell?*

"Get those spoilers down!" She roared, hanging onto the stick for dear life.

Realizing his error at last, Roberto slammed his hand down on the trim.

Immediately, the plane responded, leveling off at last.

"Orbis two-two-four-zero...come in Orbis two-two-four-zero!"

It was Fiumicino Tower squawking at her through the headset. No wonder they sounded frantic. Back in the control room at Leonardo da Vinci airport, it probably looked as if the jet had dropped off of the radar screen.

It very nearly had. Kate sucked in a chest full of air and held it, struggling to calm herself. At last she spoke. "This is Orbis two-two-four zero. Sorry for the scare, Fiumicino," she cast a warning glare at Roberto. The Italian's face was deeply reddened. "We're preparing for final approach and landing." *Preferably on a runway and not in the Tyrrhenian Sea!* The pilot grimaced.

"Roger, Orbis two-two-four-zero. Proceed on your current heading."

"Sorry," Roberto's eyes were lowered.

Kate Phillips released a long and weary sigh. She could see the Italian coast looming on the horizon, felt she could touch the tender grades of distance rising up, the hills, trees, settlements. Though she could not see it, she knew Rome was there. Somewhere.

The pilot would have no second chance here. She didn't trust the already low readings on the fuel display, and she knew the overly stressed plane would give her one shot for a landing—that was it. She'd learned early on in flight school that a good landing was the product of a good approach, and if the approach for her wounded plane went sour...well, she didn't want to think about that right now. Too many people were depending upon her.

She turned to the embarrassed Italian. "Look, that could have happened to anybody," she said through gritted teeth, "We're all under a lot of pressure." *God...what am I doing, consoling a hijacker?* A pause, and then, "I'm going to need your help landing this plane, Roberto, okay?"

He lifted his green eyes to gaze straight out the windscreen, towards land, and nodded a 'yes,' even as his lower lip trembled.

"You can do it," Kate gave his shoulder a squeeze, "I know you can. Just do as I say, when I say it, and we'll be fine!"

"*Si, bella*," Roberto ran a hand through his dark, curly hair and turned to her. "For you, I try!" and he smiled gamely.

"Good!" Kate returned his grin, and settled back in her seat. She lifted up the armrests, giving herself an unencumbered range of motion. "Here we go."

As gently as she could, using the sluggish manual controls, she began to nudge the plane into a controlled descent. Grimly, she tried not to notice how that awful rattling sound began once more.

Rome's Fiumicino airport was actually located about 18 miles northwest of the city, just east of the coastline. A few miles to the south of the airport, always visible to the pilot when she approached Rome from the west, was the city's ancient seaport of Ostia Antica. From the first time she'd seen it in flight, the pilot had felt a comfortable familiarity with the place, now in ruins, though she'd never been there. Tall pines surrounded it, waving in gentle ocean breezes; its well-preserved temples, warehouses, and the Forum reached spindly, crumbly fingers to the sky.

Closer...closer the big plane flew, so near to the water now that Kate thought for sure that they must be leaving a wake behind them. Timing the touchdown of the balky aircraft was everything now.

Out the front windscreen, the fields surrounding the airport were in full view; more pines, brush, and dusty roads. How golden and green it all appeared, in the transparent early-morning light!

It all came down to this. To her. Did she still have what it took? The harbor of Ostia had been clogged and silted up with tidal mud a millennium ago. With no other use for the city, the Romans had abandoned it...left it to ruin. Would she be able to summon, from deep within herself, the tools she never thought she'd have need of again? Soon, she would find out the answer to that question.

"Wheels down," Kate dared not remove her hands from the shimmying control column.

Roberto's fingers skipped over the displays before finding the proper buttons.

"Wheels..." a low, groaning sound reverberated through the plane, "...down." He released a relieved gust of air.

Good. Now they had something they could land on. Kate only hoped the wheels would hold up under the weight of the damaged plane. They would smack onto the ground hard and fast. Although the Italians had set aside their longest runway—14,000 feet—for the big Orbis 777-200, she feared she would need every inch of it.

"Orbis two-two-four-zero to Fiumicino Tower, are we cleared for landing?" *Like they could actually say 'no,'* the pilot ironically chuckled to herself.

*"Orbis two-two-four-zero, you are cleared,"* came the accented, faceless male voice.

"Roger that," Kate replied. "We'll see you on the ground."

The plane was rocking from side-to-side, and Kate could feel the air pressure building beneath the wings and fuselage. The runway was dead ahead, but they were coming in too damn fast, and there was nothing the pilot could do about it. She dared not risk another stall. And aborting the landing was out of the question.

Kate picked out a spot on the runway, about a third of the way down. As good a spot as any for touchdown. "Partially deploying flaps," she called out, knowing from the excitement earlier that at least these still worked.

"Too steep!" Roberto's eyes bulged at the runway—they were skimming along its surface now, barely 50 feet u— and a sharp burst of wind yawed the plane to the left.

*"Vaffanculo!"* The Italian cursed.

"Throttle back!" Kate wrenched at the knob, while at the same time madly trying to keep the plane on course. With the power cut, their speed bled away, but not fast enough.

"Damn!" Kate swore she could see the pores in the concrete surface. "Not yet." She hadn't finished rounding off the attitude of the plane. The last thing she wanted to do was to slam onto the runway nose-first. The results could be disastrous. "Fully extend flaps!" Kate ordered, and Roberto complied while she worked the ailerons and control column for all she was worth.

"Get...up...you...bastard!" The stick was back as far as it would go, and in her mind, Kate was out in front of her plane, forcibly shoving the damn nose up. The roar of the engines were diminishing, but the din in the pilot's head was off the scale. She could hear the silent screams of the passengers behind her...the quaking of an aircraft that threatened to fall apart around her...and the siren in her mind that told her she had no right to be the savior of these people.

*Focus!*  She gasped, holding the stick in a death-grip, *You can do this!*

In a great, grinding crash, the undercarriage wheels smashed onto the runway, blowing several tires out instantly.

It sounded to Kate like cannon fire, ripping away at the bottom of the plane, and she flinched in spite of herself.

A fraction of a second later, the nose-wheel hit, shoving the pilot forward in her seat. The wind was knocked out of her with the force of the hard landing, and she could feel the sweat trickling down her back as she silently begged the nose wheel to hold under the tremendous pressure.

It did.

*Not pretty, but I'll take it,* Kate thought. The plane hurtled down the runway in a barely controlled slide, rocking from side to side, nearly pitching over once. But the air currents were helping now, pressing against the fuselage and the underside of the wings and flaps, slowing it down.

"Braking..." The pilot hit the screeching wheel brakes well in advance of when she normally would have, but she didn't want to take any chances with running out of taxiing room.

It looked like a field of wetlands lay just beyond the runway, Kate could see it now, clearly. Sweat was flowing freely down her face, and her coal-black hair had long since sprung free from the orderly plait she'd featured the day before.

*Brake...lift...*she could see the water reeds waving in the breeze... *brake...lift...* There! The orange disc of a morning sun slipped free from the horizon's grasp, released to begin its timeless, inexorable march across the sky...*brake...* Would Bill and Hanson ever live to see it?

Catherine could scarcely believe it herself when, with a final, heaving gasp, the big jet finally ground to a stop. She imagined she could see the smoking glow of the deflated wheel carriage beneath her, as the efficient Fiumicino fire and emergency vehicles sprinted to the end of the runway. The 777-200 sat there, a bit the worse for the wear, like a migrating duck who'd lost its way.

A *thunk!* next to her, and Kate turned to see Roberto slumped over in his seat, fainted dead away. Well, he'd earned the right, the pilot figured.

The wails of the emergency vehicles were nearly upon them now, but the pilot reveled in the quietness of the flight deck, in the solitude that was hers, for the moment. She turned her blue eyes out towards the rising sun and released a deep, liberating breath, letting it take away from her some of the burden she'd been shouldering. It felt good to let it go.

Kate reached out to the comm switch and was surprised to see her hand shaking, as though it were not her own. Still, she forced it to do its work. "Orbis two-two-four-zero to Fiumicino tower... touchdown."

\* \* \* \* \* \* \* \* \* \*

Some things you're just better off not knowing, Captain Catherine Phillips considered. Like the minor fact that there was a gaping tear nearly 12 feet long running horizontally down the fuselage, in the area of the starboard LD-3 cargo container. A haystack of wires, singed insulation and jammed pieces of luggage, butted up against the skin of the airframe. The metal looked as though it had been peeled aside by a can opener.

Catherine had marveled at the sight. How had the plane even remained airborne? Whether it had anything to do with the reinforced bulkheads and toughened graphite floor beams of the big 777-200, or the intervention of a higher power, she did not know. She preferred not to think about it. Six of the total of twelve undercarriage wheels had blown out, and the plane now sat low and fat on the runway on this early spring Italian morning.

Once the emergency crews had reached the aircraft, a blur of activity and crisis management had ensued, starting with the hijackers being roughly taken into custody by the *polizia*. She'd felt the vile glares of Stefan and Alexandra on her as they were handcuffed, had their heads pushed down, and were shoved into police cars. She smiled as a still-groggy Roberto was taken away, and she made a point of getting a quick word in with Mishka before he was spirited off. "I'll do what I can," she told the young Kosovar, and she meant it.

The shaken passengers and crew were carefully helped off the plane and into the buses and vans that would take them back to the terminal. Kate's eyes scanned frantically across the tarmac, searching, and she froze when they found the spot where the injured were being briskly transferred into waiting ambulances. Her stomach lurched when she glimpsed a flash of blonde hair as Hanson was taken away on a stretcher.

To her dismay, the pilot found herself quickly surrounded by babbling Italian officials, anxious to get the details of the drama that had unfolded on the plane. An annoying paramedic kept swabbing at the cut on her head, while a local Orbis Airlines representative—a chubby young man with wide-set eyes and a prominent nose—trailed behind. The poor fellow was clearly overwhelmed and seemed to be talking to himself more than to anyone else. Periodically he cast a stunned look from Catherine to the damaged plane and back again.

Kate couldn't understand the half of what anyone was saying. Not that it mattered. That wasn't important right now. These idiots could wait.

Blue eyes watched the ambulances rolling off down the runway. *"Quale ospedale stanno andando?"* Her Italian was far from fluent, but she'd at least picked up enough to get by, thanks to her six month posting in Aviano a few years back.

*"Prego?"* The paramedic was confused.

*"L'ambulanzas!"* Kate's eyes flashed. *"Quale ospedale?!!"*

*"Ah...si, si!"* He bobbed his head in understanding. *"Mundi!"*

The pilot breathed a sigh of relief. Her crewmembers were being taken to one of the best private hospitals in Rome, Salvator Mundi. With English-speaking staff, at that.

*"Bene,"* Kate nodded. *"Prenderlo là."* And she moved towards an empty police car.

*"Che? No...no..."* The Orbis official scurried up to her, blocking her path. Frantically, he waved his arms back at the stunned officials. *"Per favore..."* How could she just walk out on them? There were interviews to be given, statements to be made!

Catherine's eyes grew cloudy. She reached down and grabbed the little man by his tie, jerking him towards her.

After dealing with those hijackers, this 'suit' would be chump change.

*"L'ospedale,"* the pilot said, her voice a low, threatening rumble. *"Presto!"* She released the bug-eyed Italian with a shove. He fell away, grabbing at his neck, gasping for air.

*"Presto...presto!"* she roared, boxing him on the side of his head.

The smack galvanized the man into action. *"Si...si...Capitano!"* He began talking rapidly to the emergency staff around him, gesturing towards the police vehicle and Kate, making the proper arrangements. Inside half a minute, the two were in the police car, streaking towards Salvatore Mundi Hospital. The Orbis representative knew enough by now to keep his mouth shut, and the pilot found herself lulled into a trance as the Italian scenery blurred by.

The hospital.

Bill Samuelson.

Rebecca Hanson.

Kate closed her eyes and breathed in deeply, fighting against the tightness in her chest, the fear in her heart, at what she might find there.

# Chapter
# 7

Waiting.  Catherine Phillips hated
waiting.  She'd never been good at it,
whether it was waiting for confirmation
that she'd gained her appointment to the
Air Force Academy, or waiting to see if
her father was going to somehow, impos-
sibly, walk back through the door of
their little home.  Telling them he wasn't
really dead.  That it had all been some
sort of mistake.

Bill Samuelson was going to be
okay.  A couple of long hours in surgery
later and the *dottore* had come out to tell
his anxiously waiting crew mates that

the older man would fully recover. He'd been lucky.

The Orbis flight crew had arrived at the hospital about a half-hour after Kate, exhausted to the bone, but needing to hear for themselves that their colleagues would make it. They had stolen sideways looks at the pilot as they waited for news...they were high, giddy with the fact that they'd survived their ordeal, and they viewed Kate with a newfound, awestruck respect at what she'd accomplished.

"Where's Dugan?" Kate asked, skimming her eyes around the waiting room.

"She quit," Joan Wetherill replied with a snort. "Good riddance, too. I heard her say something about a lawsuit—"

"Ha!" Nathan Berbick barked a harsh laugh, shaking his head. "It's *we* who should sue *her* for the cruel and unusual punishment of having to put up with her all this time!"

"Down, Sparky!" Alan Ross laughed, standing. "Save it for the lawyers."

"I'm going to give Bill's wife, Linda, a call," Joan said, rising also.

"I'm sure she'd like to hear from a friendly voice right about now."

"Good idea, Joan," Kate replied, giving the older redhead a grateful nod.

"Well, I've got to lie down before I fall down," Cindy Walter's sweet, southern accent filled the room. "What do you say, superman?" The petite woman reached a hand out to Nathan.

The dark-eyed man stood and crooked his elbow to her. "May I escort you to the Metropolis Hilton?"

"No thanks," Cindy said, yawning. "We'd have to fly there. The one in Rome will do just fine," she laughed.

"Tell Becky we'll be back tomorrow," Nathan said, ushering Cindy out into the corridor.

"Will do," Kate called after them.

Alan Ross hesitated, staring at the pilot shyly. He still looked pale under the tan of his skin. The long night had been hard on him. "Captain...are you—I mean—do you want me to, ah..."

"Get out of here, Ross." Kate lightly placed her hand on his shoulder. "Go get some sleep."

"Okay," he sighed, somewhat relieved. "Make sure Champ knows I was here."

"I will," she smiled wanly, watching the tall Californian leave.

"Catherine." It was Joan's voice, calm and low, just next to her.

"Mmmm?"

The senior flight attendant gave her a frank, level stare. "Are you okay?"

"I'm fine," the pilot replied, turning to look distractedly out the window.

"Are you sure?"

"Really...I'm fine." Kate swung back to her. "I'm just...just going to sit with Hanson for a while...so a familiar face is around in case she wakes up."

"Catherine, you heard the doctors. With that sedative they gave her, she'll probably be out of it until tomorrow!" Joan was not just a little alarmed at the picture of the Orbis captain in front of her. Dark circles were painted under her eyes, blood stained the collar of her shirt, bruises dotted the skin exposed on her arms, and her overall disheveled appearance certainly matched one who had been to hell and back. The woman looked as though she ought to be admitted to the hospital herself.

The captain said nothing. She just stared past Joan with unseeing eyes, her thoughts a million miles away.

"Catherine?"

A page blaring in over the intercom, a woman speaking in rapid Italian, roused the pilot from her reverie.

"I'm staying," she said firmly, shifting her eyes back to the senior flight attendant. "Just in case."

"Okay," Joan threw up her hands and grinned. "I tried." She turned and gathered up her flight bag, slinging it over her shoulder with a sigh. She looked back at the captain and saw that her thoughts had drifted off again. The woman was amazing, Joan considered. She never would have guessed that Catherine Phillips cared so deeply for her passengers and fellow crewmembers...way beyond the standard professional level of duty. The tall, dark woman had shown her a hell of a lot over the past 24 hours, and she wasn't likely to forget it. Ever.

"Catherine?"

"Hmmm?"

"Thanks. For everything."

"Don't mention it." The corner of Kate's mouth lifted up in a half-smile as she followed the smaller woman out of the waiting room. Without another word, she peeled away to head back down the corridor. To Hanson.

"Oh, Captain!" Joan stopped and spun around, calling after the tall, solitary figure. "Where will I be able to find you?"

Catherine replied without breaking her stride. "Here."

\* \* \* \* \* \* \* \* \* \*

She was lost. Floating, adrift in the pain...and fear. Rebecca struggled against it. She fought the panic...battled the darkness. And found that her uncertainty was replaced by confidence. A new strength imbued her from within, and yet she felt the power of it surround her, flow into her, too. Carried on the wings of a glance. The hint of a touch. She was not lost. She did not stand alone. Never alone. Such a lovely dream after all, wasn't it?

Crisp white painted walls. Blinds half-closed on the windows. Hushed, distant voices down the hall. The faint smell of antiseptic and freshly laundered sheets, and the *beep-beep* of the monitors and i.v. line. Catherine Phillips wasn't sure just how much time had passed by, sitting there watching the gentle rise and fall of Rebecca Hanson's chest as she slept. Minutes? Hours?

Kate didn't care. She had no thought of being anywhere else.

How small and frail the young woman looked, a white sheet tucked nearly to her chin...hooked up to those blasted machines! Her face was so pale, nearly blending into the whiteness of the pillow she peacefully rested on; only her feathered, golden hair retained its vibrancy in the dimmed interior of the hospital room.

What was the matter with this kid, walking onto her plane and standing up to those hijackers without giving a fig of a thought to her own safety? Barging into the cockpit and...and... Kate closed her eyes briefly against the vision of Hanson lying on the flight deck, bleeding from a bullet meant for her.

One of Rebecca's arms lay on top of the bed sheet. Impulsively, Kate reached out and took the young woman's hand in her own. She was gentle, careful not to disturb the lines running into the translucent skin. Just that simple gesture calmed the pounding in the taller woman's heart, though she was hard-pressed to know exactly why.

"Hanson," the pilot said softly to the sleeping woman, *"you* are the crazy one!"

Kate startled as the flight attendant stirred, blinking a green eye open at her.

"I *do* have a first name, you know!" she complained, and she struggled to sit up.

"Wha— take it easy there," Kate said, blushing, pulling her hand away. She swung her gaze around the room, desperate to be looking anywhere rather than at the two emerald orbs examining her curiously. "Let me get the doctor...do you want some water? Don't move...are you in any pain? I can —"

"*Captain...*" The sharpness of Hanson's voice stopped her in her tracks.

"Yes?"

"I'm fine. Really," she said, pushing herself into a sitting position.

"You're sure?" Catherine persisted, calming down. She reached behind Hanson to help her, adjusting her pillows and gently easing her back against them.

"I'm sure," Becky said with a sigh and a dismissive wave. "Heck," she scrunched up her nose, "it's like they say on television. You know...just a 'flesh wound.' I'll probably get out of here tomorrow."

"We'll see about that," Kate said archly. She offered the younger woman a sip of water through a straw, and Becky gratefully accepted it.

"What are you," she said after a few gulps, "a doctor now?"

"I have many skills," Kate replied in mock seriousness.

Becky laughed aloud. The laughter was quickly replaced by a grimace of pain that contorted her face. Her hand flew to her shoulder. "Aaah…"

"Hey, take it easy there." Kate was right at her side. "Miss 'Flesh Wound.' I'm getting the doctor." She reached for the 'call' button.

"No…please—" Rebecca flung out a hand to stop her. "I-I just want to talk a while longer, okay? I promise I'll be good!"

Catherine looked at the chalky pallor of the innocent face turned up to her, and she hesitated.

"Please?" The green eyes sparkled. So trusting. So hopeful. The pilot could not refuse her.

"Okay," she said sitting down, and Becky visibly relaxed.

"They told me Bill was gonna be okay?"

"Yeah. He will."

"Thank God." Becky wiped away an errant tear from the corner of her eye.

*Dammit, what was Hanson doing weeping again?* Catherine hated to see her cry!  "And everybody says 'hi'—they'll be back tomorrow," she quickly rushed on, hoping to put a stop to the waterworks.

It worked.

"Tell them 'hi' back from me, would you?" Becky sniffled.

"You got it.  Alan Ross in particular..."

"Aw, that sweetie!  He reminds me so much of my brother!" she smiled, and then alarm skipped over her face.  "My family..."

"Don't worry," Kate said.  "I talked to your mother a half an hour ago.  She wants you to *sleep,*" she emphasized, "and said they'll give you a call in the morning."

"Thanks."  Becky eased back, her worry evaporating like a summer sunshower.

*Nothing ventured, nothing gained,* Kate figured, continuing,  "Ahh...Alan, and the others...why do they call you 'Champ'?"

"Oh, it's silly," Becky said.  "I-I finished first in my training class.  Everybody kind of thought it was a  joke, but—"

"You should be proud of that," Kate said, her voice firm.

Becky flashed her an appreciative look. "Thanks. I was."

A nurse bustled into the room with a stethoscope draped around her neck and a blood pressure cuff in hand. She meant business.

"Ah, you are awake, Miss Rebecca!" Her voice was only lightly accented. "And how are we feeling?"

"We're just fine," Becky replied, shooting Kate a warning glare.

*"Bene...bene!"* The nurse began bustling around Becky, adjusting the drip, checking her vitals.

Catherine stood uncomfortably. "I'll just wait outside..."

"No-no-no!" the nurse clucked, pushing the pilot back down in her seat. "You can stay here with your friend."

Catherine dared not argue with the officious, buxom woman, both on the point of leaving and whether she was Rebecca's friend.

She stayed put.

"So, how's your headache?" Becky eyed her carefully as the nurse finished up and whisked out of the room.

"All gone," Kate lied.

"I don't know about that." Becky reached up her hand to lightly touch the reddened, bruised mark on the pilot's forehead. Kate was so surprised by the gesture, that she didn't have time to flinch away. "You'll have to keep an eye on it," Becky said, dropping her arm back onto the bed.

"What are you, Hanson, a doctor now?" Recovering, Kate laughed and mimicked the younger woman's earlier words.

Rebecca snorted. Green eyes flickered up to the ceiling and then swung down again, zeroing in on the tall, raven-haired woman.

"It's Becky."

"Hmmm?" Catherine arched an eyebrow, playing dumb.

"My name. My friends call me Becky." The young woman held the pilot in her gaze, knowing she was squirming under the onslaught of it. Daring her to back away.

She didn't.

Catherine stuck out a hand, feeling the warmth of a smaller one slip into her own. *"Rebecca,"* she said pointedly, smiling. "Catherine Phillips. My friends call me Kate. Pleased to meet you!" Blue eyes melted into green, as two old souls met each other again for the very first time.

*"Capitano! Capitano!"* Mario, the chubby Orbis representative, skittered into the room. Kate quickly leaped to her feet, putting herself between the red-faced Italian and Becky.

"What is it?" she hissed in a low voice.

*"Telefono!"* He waved a cellular in her face.

"Not now!" she said darkly, batting his arm away.

*"Per favore!"* he begged, his eyes shooting nervously at the phone. "Signor Vandegrift!" He stumbled over the pronunciation of the name of Orbis' director of flight operations.

Kate weakened. After all, the little Italian had done a fairly good job of keeping the press and all but the non-essential authorities out of her way. That, and the fact that she actually welcomed the sound of another friendly voice right now, made her reach for the phone.

"Give it to me," she said, grabbing it from him. She shushed the harried Mario out of the room. *"Vanno!"*

The little man scurried off.

"I won't be a minute," she smiled at Becky, taking a few steps towards the door.

She flipped open the phone. "Cyrus?"

"Great job, Katie!" The voice of her former mentor crackled through the cellular connection.

"Thanks," she said simply. "I had a lot of help."

"Delighted that everybody's going to be okay!"

"Yeah," she flashed a quick look at Rebecca, "me, too."

*"Well..."* he cleared his throat, "I've got a real tiger by the tail back here, trying to explain how those hijackers got through security...the damned strike..."

Catherine knew what was coming next. "I've got to go, Cyrus."

*"Katie, wait!"* His gruff voice was plaintive, beseeching her, across the thousands of miles. "You're a good pilot, Katie. One of the best. I don't know anyone else who could've done for us...for those people...what you did today. I don't want to lose you."

Kate gripped the phone so tightly she feared it might shatter into pieces in her hand. Dammit, why did he have to put her on the spot like this? How could she be expected to think clearly after what she'd just been through? Her thoughts were more muddled now than they had ever been.

When she'd stepped onto the jet...her jet...back on the tarmac at JFK, she thought she'd known exactly what she wanted. Now, she wasn't so sure. It had been a flight from hell, that was for sure, but, by God, she'd gotten her plane down in one piece. And that success had depended upon her executing some of the most challenging flying of her career.

People had trusted her to get the job done, and she had. Even when she hadn't been so certain of the outcome herself.

"Katie? Katie—you still there?"

"Yes, Cyrus," she said patiently, casting a sidelong look over at Becky. The late afternoon sun was filtering through the blinds, speckling ribbons of light on the young woman's face and on the bed sheet. Her eyes were beginning to droop, heavy with sleep.

"Katie, listen to me," his voice was earnest now, "I want your opinion on something."

Silence.

"You see, it's about this letter that was delivered to me," he continued. "It was a mistake, I think." A pause and then, more softly, "What do you think?"

Kate waited for the thousands of reasons she had for leaving to leap into her mind. After all, she had been thinking about it for weeks. Months, even. Attacked the subject from every angle, turning it inside out and upside down. Finally she had convinced herself, thanks to her exhaustive personal inventory, that she was doing the right thing.

But in the final analysis, right here, right now, standing in Rebecca Hanson's hospital room, for the life of her, she couldn't think of what a single one of those damned reasons were.

She sighed, resting her blue eyes on Rebecca. "Yeah," she said quietly. "It was a mistake."

"I knew it!" Cyrus boomed into the line, and Kate could almost hear the smile in his voice. "Take some time off, Katie," he added excitedly. "No rush to get back here. Rest up. See the sights for once, why don't you? You know, there's this thing called the 'Colosseum'..."

"Knock it off, Cy," Catherine chuckled. "I get your drift!"

"See you when you get back then, okay?"

"Sure," she paused and then plunged ahead. "Thanks, Cy. Your faith in me...it really means a lot." But the static hum of the connection told her that the older man had signed off. He hadn't heard.

*Just as well,* Catherine thought, snapping the phone shut. *Wouldn't want him to think I was going all soft on him!*

"That was Mr. Vandegrift?" Hanson asked in a sleepy voice.

"Yeah," Kate moved back to her bed-side and sat down. "He just wanted to touch base with me...wants me to take a few days off...."

"Really?" Rebecca brightened. "Captain...er...Kate," the name sounded comfortable rolling off her tongue, "you know, I'm sure I'll get sprung from here tomorrow. I-I had planned on taking a few days off myself, you know, hanging out at a *pensione*, sightseeing, stuff like that!"

"Oh?" Kate kept her voice even, her face unreadable. Did this girl know what she was saying? Perhaps it was the medication she was on. Surely, she had better things to do than spend time with an irritable ex-Air Force pilot!

"Of course," Becky blushed deeply and turned her face to the window, "you've probably seen the sights here a million times." She fidgeted with a frayed edge of her bed sheet. "Or...maybe you have some other plans..." her voice trailed off.

Kate was stunned. The young Californian actually wanted to be in her company. The pilot wasn't too sure how she felt about it. It had been so long since she'd allowed herself to get close to anyone and she wasn't sure she wanted to now. *Ah...what the hell.* There was something about the kid...and anyway, it would give her a good opportunity to keep an eye on her.

"Flesh wound" or not, she was concerned about Hanson's close call. No matter what the doctors said, it wasn't a very smart idea for the young woman to be off on her own so soon after such an injury. She would need time to recover fully. She was a part of Catherine's crew, and the pilot figured she was responsible for the flight attendant.

"You saved my life," Kate said, quietly. "That was a dumb risk you took."

"I know." Becky faced her, sheepishly. "But it seemed as good a time as any to take a chance."

"Now where have I heard *that* before?" Kate said, her blue eyes laughing.

"I wouldn't know," Becky cheekily replied.

"It's obvious you need someone around to keep you out of trouble," the pilot resolved, squaring her shoulders. "And I know a place on the Via Veneto where you can buy those T-shirts and miniatures you wanted..."

Becky's eyes flew open wide, with an understanding of what this striking, bronze-skinned woman was implying. "And there's a place near the Vatican where I hear the manicotti is fantastic!" she enthused.

"You can keep your manicotti. But if they've got a nice veal chop..."

"I'm sure they do!"

"Then you're on!" Kate couldn't resist; she reached out and ruffled the little blonde's hair.

"This is gonna be great!" Becky smiled, yawning.

"Okay now, time for you to get some sleep," Kate said sternly, tucking the covers in around the younger woman.

"All right," Becky conceded, feeling the strength of the sedative regaining control over her worn out body.

"Do...do you mind..." her eyelids were at half-mast now, "just waiting until I fall asleep? I know it's silly, but—"

"It's okay, I'll be here," the pilot said, clasping her hand.

Satisfied with that response, it was only a matter of moments before Rebecca's breathing once again became deep and even. In the dying afternoon light, Kate thought the young girl looked like an angel.

The pilot lifted her eyes towards the window. Through the blinds, she could see the blue skies overhead, a stand of pines outside the hospital dipping in the breeze, a sparrow flitting by. Though the sun was about to set, Catherine thought that her prospects had never seemed so bright.

Her long night was over.

Somehow, some way, the darkness had lifted.

Kate swung her gaze back down to the peacefully slumbering Rebecca Hanson. For whatever reason, the younger woman trusted her.

Completely.

Catherine Phillips did not plan on letting her down.

"Don't worry," she whispered softly to the sleeping form. "I'm not going anywhere."

Don't miss the continuing story of Captain Phillips and Becky Hanson—in these sequels from Yellow Rose Books...

## Roman Holiday (available now)

Orbis airlines pilot Catherine Phillips decides to spend a layover in Rome with Rebecca Hanson. The two women are soon caught up in the magical splendor of the Eternal City, seeing the sights and drawing ever-closer to one another in the process.

## Storm Front (available Spring 2001)

From the moment she receives a middle of the night phone call notifying her of a downed passenger jet, Captain Catherine Phillips, director of Orbis Airlines' new strategic operations unit, finds herself drawn deeper and deeper into the dark, dangerous world of international terrorism. Aided by a reliable investigative team including flight attendant Rebecca Hanson, Catherine quickly realizes the evidence from the terrible crash points to one terrorist in particular, a zealot who will stop at nothing to achieve his fundamentalist ends. In a cat and mouse game that spans the globe, Kate and Becky soon find themselves caught up in a desperate race against time, and the odds, where they must fight to hang onto one another, as well as their very lives.

Other titles to look for in the
coming months from
RENAISSANCE ALLIANCE PUBLISHING, INC.


**Chasing Shadows**
By C. Paradee

**Forces of Evil**
By Trish Kocialski

**Out of Darkness**
By Mary Draganis

**And Those Who Trespass Against Us**
By H. M. Macpherson

**You Must Remember This**
By Mary Draganis

**Silent Legacy**
By Ciarán Llachlan Leavitt

**Vendetta**
By Talaran

A lover of travel and adventure all her life, Belle (Bel-wah) Reilly currently lives in southeastern Pennsylvania, where she enjoys a somewhat less perilous existence than the exciting characters she creates. "It's been a really fun process for me, " Belle says, "with each new story, seeing what interesting direction Catherine and Rebecca will go in, and what the next 'curve in the road' will be for them. One thing's for sure: those ladies always get in the last word!"

Printed in the United States
54033LVS00001B/52-54